BOUNCING BETTY

THE SCARLET CHRONICLES

LILIANA HART

To Ava - I'm so proud of the woman you've become. When I write strong women characters I think of you. I love being your mom.

ACKNOWLEDGMENTS

Getting a book out is a huge task that takes an amazing team. Thanks to my cover designer, Dar Albert at Wicked Smart Designs for knocking it out of the park with these gorgeous covers. Thanks to my editors, Imogen Howson and Ava Hodge, for always making my books better. And last, but not least, thanks to Scott Silverii for being the best partner, husband, sounding board, and all-around "get stuff done" guy. I love you like crazy.

Genetics were a heck of a thing to Scarlet Holmes's way of thinking.

The little girl hopped out of the black sedan, wobbling slightly with the weight of her backpack on her shoulders. More than ninety years spanned between their ages, but it was like looking in a mirror. At least, the mirror of her childhood.

The driver closed the door behind the small child and then gave Scarlet a staunchly disapproving look before rounding the car and getting back behind the wheel. Charles was an old busybody, and she knew he'd report his findings to his employer. Not that she was doing anything wrong. An old lady couldn't even sit on her front porch swing and drink lemonade anymore without someone running off to tattle.

Scarlet narrowed her eyes as the little girl kept her head down and took in a heaving sigh before starting what looked like a death march down the long drive.

"Ada Mae Dempsey," Scarlet called out, her voice echoing like a drill sergeant. "Light a fire under those feet. I could die before you get here."

Ada picked up the pace, but she didn't lift her head. She kicked at invisible rocks and looked so pitiful Scarlet had to stifle a laugh. And then the girl finally made her way up the steps of the big white house that had been in her family for generations.

"Well, look what the cat dragged in," Scarlet said, trying not to let her worry show.

She scooted her way to the edge of the swing so her thick-soled white sneakers touched the wooden slats of the porch, and she waited until the swing was moving forward before hopping off. The skirt of her bright yellow sundress clung to the back of her legs. Whiskey Bayou in August was like sitting in a bowl of hot soup. As old as she was, if she wasn't careful, her skin would fall off the bone like a soup chicken.

"As much as I like looking at the top of your head," Scarlet said, "a Holmes always faces the music. We hold our chins up high, even if you've got five or six of them like my great-aunt Gertie."

Ada let her backpack slip off her shoulders and it hit the porch with a thud, and then she tightened her little fists and lifted her chin defiantly. Scarlet's lips twitched. Ada Mae was a chip off the old block all right.

Lordy, she was a mess. Her dark pigtails were whompyjawed, her white uniform shirt was missing a button, her knees were skinned, and one of her argyle socks drooped to her ankle. She looked pitiful.

"Hmmph," Scarlet said. "It looks like school hasn't changed much since I was there."

"They had school when you were a kid?" Ada asked, wide eyed.

"They sure did," she said. "But I looked way worse than you. I went to an all-girls school. Girls really know how to pull hair."

Ada might have had her father's piercing blue eyes, but she was a Holmes through and through. Ada rubbed at her scalp and grinned, the single dimple in her cheek identical to the one in Scarlet's.

"Yeah, but that stuff you taught me came in real handy. Paris Wheeler's thumb bent back really far, and she screamed *really* loud."

"Paris Wheeler is a second grader," Scarlet said, surprised. "Since when did they start putting kindergarten and second grade on the playground together?"

Ada's grin disappeared and she got that

stubborn set to her chin that said she'd already shared too much. "I smell cookies."

"Verna made them fresh to celebrate your first day of school. Better go get one before I eat them all. Girls that fight with second graders maybe don't deserve a lot of cookies."

Ada took a minute to measure her mark, and her lip quivered as her eyes started to fill.

"You know that's wasted on me," Scarlet said. "If you're going to sell it you've got to get rid of the mad in your eyes."

"Works on everybody else," Ada grumbled under her breath and headed toward the little table next to the swing. She daintily selected a chocolate-chip cookie, and Scarlet poured her a cup of lemonade from the glass pitcher. She waited until Ada climbed up into the swing and spread a napkin across her lap before Scarlet handed her the cup. Then she took the seat next to her and started the swing rocking.

"How come tears work on everyone but you?" Ada asked.

"Because everyone else is a bunch of suckers. I got tortured by Nazis. Takes a lot more than a quivering lip to break me."

Ada let out a long-suffering sigh and took another bite of cookie, and then she looked at it as if it wasn't doing the job, making Scarlet's lips twitch again.

"Mama always says when days are really bad it's best to go straight to the ice cream."

"Who do you think taught your mama that? Have a cookie now, and we'll have ice cream for dessert after dinner. You've got to learn to pace yourself."

"Hmm," Ada said, and pressed her lips together.

Scarlet grabbed a couple more cookies for herself and settled back, listening to the swing creak and the fans whir lazily overhead.

"So," Scarlet said. "How was school? Learn anything new?"

"Not really," Ada said, letting out a very adult sigh. "I knew it all already. I don't think school is going to work out. We should look for alternatives."

Scarlet's brows rose in surprise. "That would probably surprise your parents when they get back from their trip. I'm not sure there's a lot of alternatives for five-year-olds in this area. Back in my day you'd be working in the fields or sewing until your little fingers bled."

"I'm more management material," Ada said.

Scarlet barked out a laugh and then she nodded at Ada solemnly, giving her a conspirator's wink. "It's lonely at the top. My parents didn't much know what to do with me either."

"I don't think Mama and Daddy are going

to be too happy with me," Ada said. "I told Ms. Perkins not to bother calling them because they're trying to have a getaway before the baby comes, but I could tell she wasn't listening. The old busybody."

Scarlet stifled a snort as Ada mimicked her thoughts about the driver earlier, and then she tried to make her face stern. "That's not a very respectful thing to say about your teacher."

"No, I suppose not," Ada said heaving another sigh. "But the way I see it, a school like Primrose Academy is never going to help me relate to the common man. I need to be in the trenches."

"Well, from the looks of it, you spent the day in the trenches. Are you going to tell me what happened, or am I going to get a phone call from someone later?" Scarlet asked.

If possible, Ada's lips tightened even more, and she got that stubborn line between her eyes that Scarlet had seen in her own reflection on more than one occasion.

"It was just a difference of political opinion," Ada said. "I tried to handle it with my words like you said, but Paris Wheeler took offense at being told she had as much empty space between her ears as her daddy for backing that bill in the senate. I guess she didn't get the memo that we're supposed to settle disputes with our words because before I could say anything else she had me by the hair and was sitting on my chest. She's put on a pound or two over the summer."

"I'm guessing you told her that too," Scarlet asked, not sure whether to scold her or ask what happened next.

"It wasn't one of my finer moments," Ada said. "She just got me so mad talking about Daddy that way. She said he was any empty-headed dunderhead.

Scarlet nodded in agreement. "It's important to defend your family and the people you love. It's how you go about defending them that's important. You've got to keep a cool head in times like these."

"Did you always keep a cool head when defending your family?" Ada asked.

"Lord no," Scarlet said. "And it got me into some real fixes. But I never really had to defend my family growing up. You should be glad you have parents and people in your life who love you like they do. My daddy couldn't wait to boot me out the door."

"Granny says it's because you couldn't keep your legs together," Ada said, and then her face squinched up with a quizzical expression. "What does that mean?"

"It means your granny needs to stop drinking the cooking sherry from the cupboard and mind her own beeswax," Scarlet said, eyes narrowed.

"So did your daddy boot you out?" Ada asked. "Daddy would never do that to me. He says me and Mama are his favorite people in the whole world."

"No, he'd never do that," Scarlet agreed. "We Holmeses are made of sturdy stock, and we don't pay much mind to the rules, but my daddy got a wild hair one day and decided to make our name more respectable. But the bayou isn't known for being respectable. My daddy could fight and drink with the best of them, but he had a real keen business mind."

Ada nodded her head with the wisdom of someone far past her years.

"He had a partner named James Walker, and during prohibition they used the solitude of the bayou to hide their distillery."

"What's prohibition?" Ada asked. "Is it scandalous?"

"It sure was," Scarlet said. "The government told everyone that alcohol was bad and banned anyone from making or selling it."

"I bet Granny hated that," Ada said, pursing her lips.

Scarlet's lips twitched. "I know Granny and I look like we're the same age, but she wasn't born then."

"Does that mean that your daddy broke the law?"

"Oh, yes," Scarlet said. "He and James made whiskey because the bayou had all the ingredients needed. And then they sold it all over Georgia and eventually to a bunch of other states. They made a fortune. My daddy even got shot once."

"Wow," Ada said, her eyes wide. "Did he die?"

"Nope," she said. "Holmeses are too mean to die. He just kept doing what he was doing."

"What about your mama? What did she do?"

Scarlet cleared her throat. Addison would wring her neck if she told Ada too much. Scarlet's mother had enjoyed the time her husband was away by spending his money and making sure his side of the bed stayed warm with anyone who caught her fancy.

"My mama was what you might call a socialite," Scarlet finally said. "She was beautiful, and she was real good at making people feel right at home. You see that trellis where all the roses are blooming?"

Ada leaned forward so she could get a better view. "I see it."

"There used to be a drainpipe there, and one time Daddy came home early and caught someone trying to climb up to the second floor."

"That's scary," Ada said. "Was he a robber?"

"You could say that," Scarlet said. "My daddy shot him right in the back. And then he ripped the drainpipe out so no one could climb up there again. We had to have the whole house repainted. Mama and Daddy never really got along after that, and she died a couple of years later. No one ever knew what happened to her. They found her body in the marsh and that was that. I was the oldest, so it was up to me to take care of my two brothers."

"You have brothers?" Ada asked.

"I used to," Scarlet said. "One died of scarlet fever and the other died in the war."

"That's sad," Ada said, biting her bottom lip. "So why'd you get shipped off if your daddy needed you to take care of your brothers?" she asked, a little too insightfully.

Scarlet sighed. She never thought she'd be spending her last days in the same house she'd been born in, but she'd made peace with her life over the last few years and it seemed fitting. And if, from time to time, moments of bitterness and memories of rejection snuck up on her as she roamed her childhood home, then she squashed them like bugs and moved on about her day. Besides, she'd made something of herself, and in hindsight, it had been the best thing for her. There weren't a lot of chances back in those days to get out of Whiskey Bayou.

"I guess he shipped me off because I reminded him too much of my mama," Scarlet finally said. "I was barely seventeen, and in those days, a lot of girls were already married and having babies. But I had an independent spirit, and I had good brains. That's why you should go back to kindergarten. You've got good brains too."

"I'll consider it," Ada said. "I feel better now that I've had cookies and had some time to reflect on it."

"Emotions sometimes get the better of us," Scarlet agreed. "We Holmes women are real passionate. If I'd have been a boy, Daddy would have brought me right into the family business. I'd have made a good man. You see, after prohibition ended, he partnered with James to open a legitimate business, but he also had other business interests. He loaned money to people when they had great ideas, and then he helped them get started and took part of their profits. He made even more money doing that than selling whiskey. I did all the books for him, and I could add numbers in my head faster than anybody."

Scarlet didn't bother to mention that she'd skimmed a little off the top for her trouble since Daddy never bothered to pay her. "I had already been working at the bank, so Daddy used me as a contact point for a lot of the businessmen coming and going out of Whiskey Bayou. I met some real characters. I even met a bank robber once."

"That doesn't sound like a good reason to boot you out to me," Ada said.

Scarlet cleared her throat and felt the heat in her cheeks. "Well, there were extenuating circumstances. James Walker was a very handsome and charming man, and I guess I fancied myself in love with him. He was almost thirty years older than I was, but he was just like a movie star. Everyone does foolish things when they're in love."

"I know," Ada said primly. "I watched *The Bachelor* with you the other night. Disgraceful. You didn't act like those women, did you?"

"Not quite that bad," Scarlet said. "But James wined and dined me in secret so my father wouldn't find out." Or his wife, she added silently. "But my father had a sixth sense about these things and he and James got into a horrible fight. By the time the dust had cleared, they'd split the business and I was on the next boat to France."

"Were you scared?" Ada asked, worry in her eyes.

"A little bit," Scarlet admitted. "But it was exciting too. I've always been of the mind that you can't dwell on the bad things in life because that just keeps you tethered to the past. Know what I mean?"

"Not really," Ada said, kicking her Mary Janes back and forth. "But I trust you."

"That's a relief," Scarlet said.

"Did you get kicked out of Paris too?" Ada asked.

"No, they loved me in Paris. It's a different culture. And they were not so uptight as the people in a small town tend to be. For me, it was a place to start over. Though the timing could have been better. I'd barely gotten off the boat before the Nazis occupied Marseille. That was a real humdinger. I'd hardly unpacked my bags before I had to kill a man."

Ada gasped and sat up straight in the swing. "Is that true? Granny says you say that a lot. She says you like to embellish."

"Granny is full of helpful information, isn't she?" Scarlet asked. "But it's true. In fact, I killed him with this very knife."

Scarlet dug into the pocket of her sundress and pulled out a small sheath knife. Ada covered her mouth with her hands dramatically.

"This was my father's," Scarlet said. "It was the only thing he gave me when I left home."

"Does it still have blood on it?" she asked.

"I cleaned it real good," Scarlet assured her. "A little bleach takes care of a lot of evidence. Something to remember."

Ada nodded. "Who'd you kill?"

"Well, that's a little more complicated," she

said, pulling the knife from the worn leather sheath. The blade was old, but just as sharp and capable as it had been the day she'd gotten it. "It's probably best if I start from the beginning…"

CHAPTER 1

Marseille, 1940

I'd always considered growing up on the bayou to be somewhat of an obstacle regarding my ability to climb up the social ladder. Polite society didn't have much use for a woman who could shoot a wild hog at a hundred paces, and they certainly didn't have much use for a woman who spoke her mind and was creative with her vocabulary.

I'm not sure what I expected after being relocated across the ocean, but it turned out all the things that were an obstacle back home came in handy on foreign soil. I was a real asset. At least to the Resistance. The other guys had a price on my head.

I'd only had one goal when I'd gotten off the ship in Marseille, and that was to find a husband. A woman on her own would always face obstacles, which was ridiculous to my mind, so I had a strategy. I needed to find a wealthy, older man who was set in his ways and had his own interests. That way, I could live the life I'd become accustomed to and do whatever I wanted at the same time. It was a win-win in my book. He didn't even have to be good looking. I'd just make sure to turn the light off before we made love and have a separate bedroom the rest of the time. It was a real sacrifice, but one I was willing to make.

I think there's a saying about *best laid plans…* because by the time I'd gotten settled with my hosts—a George and Esther Smithers, who were British citizens living half the year in France—they'd decided I was exactly what was needed to fight the Nazis.

I couldn't say for sure if I was the best weapon against the Nazis, but it was the first time in seventeen years I'd felt like I was in a place where I belonged. They didn't care about my age or that I was a woman. They didn't make me feel guilty for being able to memorize documents and numbers and information better than the men, and they didn't make me feel like I had to cover up my natural beauty. And it turned out I had a real gift for languages.

As luck would have it, there were a lot of older men in the Resistance, so I figured finding a husband would be like shooting fish in a barrel. What I hadn't expected was to hit a potential husband with my car. But in my defense, he was in my territory.

The Smitherses thought my best cover was selling makeup. A little lipstick could go a long way in getting a man to fall to his knees or a woman to share her secrets. My job was to do both of those things. And let me tell you, it wasn't an easy task because the women in the Gestapo weren't exactly *Cover Girl* material.

When the Nazis had occupied Marseille at the beginning of June, the Alliance had already been in place for some time at Number 1 Dorset Square, and in two short months I'd seen things I'd never have imagined. But they'd needed more boots on the ground, and my American status enabled them to trust me more than some of their European counterparts. Double agents and Nazi sympathizers had already been rooted out and executed in London and Paris. So I was fast-tracked into the spy game.

I had to say, I was born for it.

The Smitherses were wealthy, and they'd loaned me a car for my makeup business. I carried cases in the trunk and made my way down the avenue, stopping at everything from the perfumery to the sewing factory to the offices with bored secretaries. And then I made my way to the strategically placed locations all over the city where the Gestapo had commandeered the homes of people they'd taken into custody.

In all honesty, I might have been busy looking at the sky and the position of the sun rather than the road in front of me, but I wanted to make sure I was back to the Smithers' house before curfew. I would be cutting it close.

It's not like I was driving fast, but in my experience, men could overexaggerate things like this. And really, he came out of nowhere.

There was a blur of gray and a loud grunt, and the car jerked as it made contact. I looked to the end of the long hood and I slammed my foot on the brake, but whatever I'd hit was no longer standing.

"Shoot," I mumbled, throwing open the car door. "Who could possibly be this stupid?"

We were right in front of the Gestapo head-quarters, and drawing attention to ourselves wasn't the wisest course of action. They knew me and were used to having me stop by once a week. I'd made relationships with several of the women, and I flirted with all of the guards, but I'd especially made my availability known to a man named Friedrich Wagner, who was the head of the secret police that had been sent in to occupy Marseille.

My hard-soled shoes made scraping sounds across the cobblestone roads, and I hurried to the front of the car, hoping I could get whatever it was up and on its way with little fanfare. But I was like a beacon in my new red dress, a dress I'd purposely chosen because I knew I'd cross paths with Friedrich today and his favorite color was red. I didn't want to toot my own horn, but people tended to notice me even without the red dress. There was a reason I'd been shipped to another country, and I couldn't help it if men lost their faculties around me. We all have gifts. I just know how to use mine.

I saw the back of him first. He was dressed in a long gray overcoat, and his hat was black and cocked crookedly on his head. His shoulders were broad and hunched as he hugged his leg, and I looked back and forth down the avenue, noting the curious looks of one of the officers stationed on the sidewalk.

I gave him a full wattage smile and saw his posture relax a bit, and I knew we'd only have seconds before he made his way over to us. I was positive I could get myself out of the situation, but I wasn't so confident for my new friend.

"*Monsieur*," I said, leaning down and grabbing his arm. My French was more than adequate after two months in Marseille. "You must get up and walk away." And then I gasped softly as his gaze met mine.

I recognized him, though we'd never been formally introduced. It was impossible not to know Henry Graham. He'd moved between

England and France since the war started, collecting intelligence, and he had so many aliases the Germans weren't sure what his real name was. I wasn't even sure that Henry Graham was his real name. What I did know was that his work was too important for him to be looked at too closely.

He was handsome in a unique way. His features were sharp and angled, and I wasn't sure of his true nationality, though the British claimed him, but his crystalline blue eyes and dark blond hair could have placed his origins in many European countries.

He must have noticed the recognition in my eyes, because he took my hand and squeezed, and then said, "It will be okay."

I scanned his body quickly for any obvious signs of injury and winced as I saw the tear in his trousers and the blood seeping from a long scrape down his shin. He was dressed like many of the businessmen in the district—in a jacket and tie—his shoes polished and a thin scarf hanging jauntily from around his neck.

"Are you all right?" I asked, my voice elevated for our audience. "Can I take you somewhere? To the doctor?"

"*Oui*," he said. "I would appreciate your assistance." I moved to put my hand under his arm and get him to his feet, but the officer I'd smiled at had made his way to us. I could see my reflection in the polished shine of his boots.

He spoke in clipped German, and I only caught part of what he was saying. I didn't recognize the dialect, and I wasn't as proficient in my German as I was French, but I caught the gist and the tone.

He reached down and grabbed Graham by the arm and pulled him to his feet, causing him to stumble and keep his weight off his leg.

"I'd hate for you to trouble yourself," I said, before the officer could damage Graham any further. "This was my fault, and I'm happy to take him to the doctor."

"Do you know this man?" the officer asked.

"Oh, no," I said, fluttering my lashes and blushing prettily. "We've never met. I'm just such a klutz and I couldn't help but admire the blue of the sky and the sun shining over the water. I wasn't paying attention to the road at all, and I ran right into this poor man. I've not seen you here before. Major Wagner and Helene are expecting me."

I'd learned from an early age that if you acted helpless around men it made them feel like the king of the world, so they'd usually try to swoop in and take over. I smiled coyly and let the smallest bit of interest linger in my eyes.

"I'm fine," Graham cut in. "No need for a doctor. It's just a cut. Please."

Graham's smile was grim but insistent. I could tell he was ready to be on his way though I was curious as to why he would chance cutting through to his destination so close to headquarters when there was a price on his head.

"We have a doctor inside," the officer said, giving Graham a hard stare. "Come."

My insides were frozen, but there was no choice but to play it out, so I got back behind the wheel and moved the car closer to the sidewalk, and then I got my cases out of the trunk.

"That's very kind of you," I told the officer, giving him an oblivious smile. "And now I get to keep my appointment. I just hate getting behind schedule."

The officer was ushering a limping Graham toward the door of Gestapo headquarters, and I resisted the urge to blow out a sigh of impatience. We were in a fix that I didn't know how to get out of, and I was hoping that Graham had a plan I hadn't thought of.

Major Wagner had commandeered the residence of the Schwartz family after they'd transported all of the Jews out of the city. Their home was considered upper middle-class, as Mr. Schwartz had been a jeweler, but it was the location that held the appeal for the Germans. It was on the corner of the Quai de Rive Neuve and it had perfect visibility of the port and the main avenue in Marseille.

I noticed passersby on the street were hurrying along, keeping their heads down, but I could feel them watching us. Another officer came out the front door and gave Graham a narrowed stare, taking in the gash in his leg and his disheveled attire.

"Lovely to see you, Heinz," I told him in German, and he gave me a tight-lipped smile. For Heinz, that was as good as him declaring his undying devotion.

He came and took my cases, sparing a glance for my bosom before ushering me into the building. There was something about the shell of the home that sent prickles of unease across my skin. It was a ghost of a house, the remnants of its former owners a memory that hadn't quite faded.

Most of the furniture had been removed, and there were faded patches on the wall where paintings had once hung. The rugs had been rolled up and the floors exposed. I knew from my intel that only Major Wagner and Dr. Meissner used headquarters as their temporary home, along with the guards who were on duty during the night.

The excitement from outside had brought Major Wagner downstairs and away from his office. I had yet to be able to access his office, but I had high hopes in that regard as long as I was able to keep him romantically interested.

Wagner stood at attention, his uniform starched and stiff, the red band vibrant around his left sleeve.

"Friedrich," I said, cutting through the quiet tension. He'd given me permission to use his first name weeks ago, but I'd been careful in using it too soon. I wanted to keep his interest and make him curious about me at the same time. I wanted to exude seduction, but also display a youthful naïveté a man like Wagner would consider a challenge.

I put a low purr in my voice when I said his name, and his attention was drawn to me instead of Graham. "I apologize for my tardiness. I know I could've waited until tomorrow to come, but I was looking forward to seeing you and thought it was worth risking curfew." I fluttered my lashes prettily, and the stone expression on his face softened.

He was an attractive man, tall and thin, his skin pale and his blond hair cut short beneath his officer's cap. He was somewhere in his late thirties or early forties, and his eyes were the color of the cognac Mr. Smithers had after dinner every night.

He stepped forward and took my hand, bending down sharply to kiss it. When he stood back up, he didn't release me.

"I'm glad you came," he said. "I propose you go upstairs and tend to your business with

Helene. She is waiting for you. And while you attend to business, I will arrange a supper for the two of us." His smile was cunning and made my skin crawl, but I lowered my eyes bashfully and he seemed to appreciate that. "No need to worry about curfew." He gave me a conspirator's wink as if he'd told a hilarious joke. "And then I will make sure you are returned home safely. My word of honor."

My smile was genuine because it was exactly the kind of invitation I'd been hoping to get for weeks.

"I'd like that very much," I said. "And I do apologize for the chaos I've caused. And now your doctor will have to be put out by tending to this man's wounds. I know how busy he is, but I'm sure Dr. Meissner will do an excellent job and have him on his way quickly."

It was common knowledge that Dr. Meissner spent his time doing horrid experiments on those who'd been captured, and the rumor was that there was a small handful of prisoners locked somewhere in the building. I'd yet to narrow down what floor they were being held on, or if they were even here at all.

I was hoping the power of persuasion would be enough to make Friedrich think twice about doing harm to Graham, but his expression hardened as he took in the Alliance's number one operative.

"Of course, my dear," Wagner said, patting me on the hand dismissively. And then he turned to the officer who'd met us on the street. "Josef, let's not make him wait any longer for treatment. Take him to my office and send for the doctor. You know where he is."

Josef nodded and pushed against Graham's back, moving him toward the stairs and Wagner's office. I snuck one last glance at Graham as he was led away, but his face was impassive. I couldn't help but think that I'd just sentenced the most wanted spy in Europe to his death.

CHAPTER 2

George and Esther Smithers' home was along the bustling Quai des Belges, facing the water and the ships and boats that were no longer allowed to leave or enter port. It was only two blocks from Gestapo headquarters, though much more opulent than the modest home they'd commandeered from the Schwartz family.

They'd given me the guest quarters on the third floor, and I was mostly left to my own devices, with the occasional interruption from my maid, Margueritte, who was barely a year or two older than I was. We got on well enough, but I was used to doing for myself, and I could tell we hadn't shared the same life experiences.

The Smitherses' home was four stories and as ornate and lavish as the other homes on the street. The walls were covered in beautiful silk wallpapers in vibrant colors, and gold leaf embellished everything. I wasn't exactly sure what George Smithers did for a living, but I figured if he knew my father then he probably hadn't made all his money on the up-and-up.

Not that I spent much time in George's company. He was busy with the Alliance, his secret meetings, and his day-to-day business dealings. Esther, on the other hand, had become a kindred sister. She was only a decade older than I was, and she and George had never had children. That was by design, as Esther had the same outlook on marriage and being a modern woman that I did. She'd found an older wealthy husband, and she'd gotten exactly what she'd wanted—freedom. According to her, she had security and she had her choice of lovers in two countries who didn't immediately fall asleep after dessert. You couldn't ask much more than that.

Esther had waited up for me, even though I'd sent a note letting her know not to worry. She was a tall woman, several inches taller than I was, and her build was delicate and wistful. She was beautiful, with skin so pale it was almost translucent, soft gray eyes, and white-blond hair that had the slightest touch of silver so it shimmered when she wore it down.

"Your dress is still on straight," she said good-naturedly, crossing her legs so the silk of her dressing gown caught the flicker of candle-light from the oil lamp beside her. She lit a cigarette and inhaled deeply, and then exhaled a thin stream of smoke.

"Well?" she asked, arching a brow.

"He was a perfect gentleman," I said, running a hand down the side of my waist and resting it on my hip. Unlike Esther, I had curves to spare and I used them to my advantage. "But I haven't put on the full charm yet. He wanted to assure me that the people of Marseille wouldn't be harmed as long as they comply, but that anyone housing refugees would be punished severely. He hinted at the experiments Dr. Meissner was conducting, but he didn't specify who they'd selected."

"Intelligence tells us that they've taken the entire Cordier family. Their home was raided on the night of the twelfth, and there is no record they were taken to any of the camps. And no bodies have been found. The Cordiers have two sets of twins. A set of boys and a set of girls. Meissner would find that fascinating, though we don't expect him to keep the parents alive. If they still are it would be a miracle, but we hope to be able to save the children. The Cordiers are a prominent family, politically connected, but someone turned them in to the Gestapo for helping Jews and other refugees escape. They were smuggling them out on their ships."

I felt the bubble of anger I had to keep tamped down at the injustices I'd seen and heard about over the last couple of months. We were so removed from life back home, and I was ashamed how ignorant I'd been. But the rage had a permanent home inside me now, and I worked hard to keep it leashed. I couldn't imagine what would happen if it ever broke free.

"Wagner spoke of the internment camp we've been looking for," I told her.

Esther sat forward in her chair, her attention caught. "Did he tell you where?"

"On the border, outside of Vitrolles. It's small, so they're moving them out to the larger camps as quickly as they can get the trains to run. Most of them go to Bergen-Belsen and then are shipped out again.

"I knew it!" she said, stamping out the cigarette in the ashtray on the table. "What about the British Intelligence officers they captured?"

"He was happy to mention them," I said. "He said it's his mission to smoke out every traitor. There's a train leaving in two days. Our men are meant to be on it."

"You'll need to be debriefed first thing in the morning," she said, coming to her feet. "We must get those men out of France and back home. Did Wagner suspect you? What did you tell him?"

"The truth," I said, smiling coyly. "That I'm American and my father sent me to France to live with a friend so I could search for a husband. I let him know the position was still open while I fiddled with the top button of my dress."

"Men are so easy," she said.

"He wants to see me again," I said. "He might have people watching the house."

She waved her hand. "I would be surprised if he didn't. We can handle it. And everyone in the Alliance uses the secret entrance anyway. We're well protected here. Sleep tonight. You've earned it."

I wanted to ask about Henry Graham. Whether there had been any word about him. Whether or not Wagner's men had beaten him to within an inch of his life or sent him to the internment camp to wait for death with the others. But I stayed silent.

There were times this strange world seemed like a game. A game I was good at and one I couldn't possibly lose. I'd felt invincible from the start—untouchable—as if the stories I'd heard about others in the Alliance being captured and killed were mere fairy tales. But in the blink of an eye, I realized that it was real lives on the line and real consequences for stupid actions.

Graham had only been a legend in my mind, someone I'd seen from a distance a time or two. But it was his blood on my hands after today.

I bid Esther good night and promised to be up and ready in the morning. My head was spinning with the information Wagner had inadvertently leaked while we were sipping wine and flirting over dinner. I wouldn't forget it. I never forgot anything. And maybe what I'd learned tonight would save lives and make up for the one I'd potentially lost today.

By the time I reached the third-floor landing exhaustion hit. The sconces were dimmed in the hallway so I could see myself to my room. I had the third floor to myself, and I'd had to practically threaten Margueritte to get her to leave me in peace in the evenings. I'd been dressing and undressing myself for a long time and didn't need the help now. I wasn't sure if I hurt her feelings or not, but she'd left me to my peace and still left chocolates on my dresser, so I figured she wasn't too mad.

I pushed open the door to my room and breathed in the fresh scent of lilacs and baby powder. The room was large and would be drafty without the thick blue carpet and matching velvet drapes. There was a marble fireplace at the opposite end from the bed, but there was no need for a fire at this time of year, though the nights were much cooler than I was used to. I had my own bathroom and tub, and I planned to make full use of it before I met with anyone in the morning.

There was a single oil lamp on the night-stand, dimmed so only a flicker of light showed. I tossed my wrap over the back of a chair and started undoing the buttons on my dress, stopping to take the combs out of my hair because they were giving me a headache.

It wasn't until I moved to the wardrobe to get my nightclothes that I realized I wasn't alone in the room. I caught the shadow of his silhouette from the small gap in the curtains that let in a hint of moonlight.

I went about my business, reaching under my dress to undo my garters. I slipped the small knife I kept tied to my garters from the sheath and hid it under my nightclothes, and then I finished unbuttoning my dress and let it fall from my shoulders so I was dressed only in my slip. I turned and headed toward the bed, wanting to be at the best angle and distance to throw my knife and hit the target, but my plans were interrupted with the strike of a match.

I saw the flame flicker and smelled sulfur as the tip of his cigarette went red.

"I can't decide if I'd rather die from a heart attack if you take off more clothes or from that knife you're hiding," he said.

"There are worse ways to die than either

one," I told him. There was no point in covering up. We weren't children and I didn't want him to think he intimidated me. "I see you're still alive."

Henry Graham chuckled and stretched his legs out in front of him, crossing his ankles and making himself at home as if it were his room instead of mine. "I could say the same to you," he said. "You made it back from dinner in one piece. Other women haven't been so lucky."

I arched a brow. "I'm not other women." I'd been listening to the timbre of his voice and there was something there that intrigued me. "You're not British."

"It says on my papers I am," he said.

"Ah, yes," I said, moving toward him slowly so the moonlight shone on my slip, making it practically transparent. I leaned down and took a cigarette from the black case on the table, putting it between my lips and then leaning closer so he could light mine with his own. "We all have papers, don't we," I said, blowing out a stream of smoke and walking away so he could get a back view.

I had no idea what Graham was doing in my room, but I felt the challenge of matching wits with his and I wondered if he could be broken like any other man.

"You're very good," he said.

"You don't know how good."

He barked out a laugh and sat up straight, mashing out his cigarette in the ashtray.

"What did you learn from Wagner tonight?" he asked, turning from pleasure to business in the blink of an eye.

"What did you discover in his office today?" I countered. "Interesting he'd have you taken there."

I might be new to this world of intrigue, but if I'd learned anything over the past two months it's that information was sacred and in the wrong hands it could be deadly. I knew Graham only by reputation, but I liked to size a guy up before I started trading life stories.

His smile was thin this time. "Don't worry. I had my cyanide pill, just in case."

I had mine in the small locket I wore around my neck. There were two things I never left home without—my knife and a quick way to die.

"So why aren't you dead?" I asked.

"Wishful thinking?" he asked.

"Do you always answer a question with a question?" I countered. "We haven't even been properly introduced. What do you want from me?"

He arched a brow and his eyes smoldered with something more. "That's a loaded question if I've ever heard one."

Now it was my turn to laugh. "And to think

Wagner was more of a gentleman tonight than you're being."

"I've been many things in this life," he said. "But a gentleman is not often one of them."

He made his way toward me with slow deliberate steps, and I felt my heart catch in my chest. *This* was a man. And he made all the others I'd known in my life dim in comparison.

He held out his hand and I placed my smaller one in his, watching as he bent down to kiss the back of it. He lingered, gazing up to see my reaction.

"Henry Graham, at your service," he said.

I pulled my hand away slowly and gave him a look that would've had lesser men puddling at my feet. "A pleasure," I said. "Scarlet Holmes."

"Hmm, it suits you," he said. "I've heard of you, of course."

"Naturally," I said, feigning indifference, though I was curious how he'd have heard of me. My work so far had mostly been observing and gathering information. I'd done nothing spectacular to draw attention to myself.

"Codename: Bouncing Betty," he said. "You're quite infamous, you know? You have a reputation for superior intellect and heart-stopping seduction. I can see they weren't exaggerating. The Alliance has great hopes for you."

"I have great hopes for them as well," I said. "As lovely as it is to have evening guests in my bedroom, can you enlighten me as to why the great Lord Hawkeye is gracing me with his presence?" I asked, using his own codename.

"You've done well," he said. "You've managed to become one of Wagner's interests, and hopefully you'll become one of his distractions. This entire city is under his command. There is a French girl working as a maid at the Gestapo headquarters. Her name is Lise. Each week when you visit Helene she will slip a tin of makeup into your case after she delivers tea. There are coordinates inside the makeup tin and you'll take them to the next destination on your route, where someone will relieve you of them."

"Am I working for you now?" I asked.

"Get some rest," he said. "Debriefings are always long and tedious."

And then without answering any of my questions, he walked out of my room. I went to the closed door and flicked the lock, but I knew it wouldn't keep him out. I was crackling with energy and unspent tension and I knew it wouldn't be a restful night. I didn't know if Henry Graham was good husband material, but I wasn't past letting him try.

CHAPTER 3

My family didn't spend a lot of time in church back in Whiskey Bayou, but I remembered a certain sermon about pride going before destruction. I probably should have paid closer attention to that one.

I knew it was because of the information I'd provided during debriefing that had allowed agents to find the camp and liberate dozens of prisoners. On a personal note, it had eased my mind immensely to have seen Graham in the debriefing room sitting in one of the high-backed chairs.

I'd found out later that night, when he'd visited me in my room again, that he was one of the agents chosen to free the prisoners. He was a kindred spirit, and I recognized part of myself in the wildness in him. There had been excitement in his eyes at the thought of sneaking his way into enemy territory. The danger was as addicting as anything I'd ever felt.

I'd woken in the middle of the night and stretched my hand across the bed, but the sheets were cool and empty, though I could still smell his cologne on the pillow. I tried to go back to sleep, but it came in fitful spurts the rest of the night, my mind occupied with nightmares that this mission might be Graham's last.

It was a dangerous mission. But he knew the risks of the job better than anyone. The rest of that night and the day passed in a blur. And when Wagner sent roses and a note telling me he'd call on me again, for a split second, I wished they were from Graham. There was a girlish dream in my heart that the night, or half the night, we'd spent together meant as much to him as it had to me. But my experience with men had taught me not to hope too much. That way the disappointment wasn't so great.

But I was pleasantly surprised when Graham came to my room again the next night. Truthfully, it had almost been dawn. I'd been fast asleep, dreaming of his lips on mine, when suddenly, they were, and I wondered if I'd become his obsession like he'd become mine. He'd come directly from his mission in Vitrolles to me. And that had to mean something.

Our time had been short, because he'd been gone again before I'd woken the next morning, sneaking in and out of my bed like he'd snuck into my heart. When I'd finally pulled myself together and managed to get dressed and down to breakfast, I was determined and inspired to make my mark on this war like he had. Lord Hawkeye would always be known as one of the greatest spies who ever lived. I saw no reason Bouncing Betty couldn't be synonymous with his.

"You've certainly got some color in your cheeks," Esther said when I sat across from her at the breakfast table. She gave me a knowing smile as she rang the bell for the kitchen maid to bring in my breakfast.

"Hmm," I said, unable to keep the grin from my face.

George had left the morning paper folded on the table. It had been freshly ironed, though there were smudges of ink where he'd turned the pages.

There was no truth in the newspapers, only propaganda that the Nazis wanted the people to see. The best way to control people was to keep them in fear. But the Alliance read the papers faithfully, ferreting out nuggets of truth amid the deceptions.

I nibbled on toast as I scanned the pages until I saw what I was looking for.

"The train is coming in from Paris tomorrow with new supplies," I told Esther. "I should send

Helene a note and let her know. She always likes
to be the first to see what's new from Paris. And
I need to move faster and have more opportunities inside their headquarters. Once a week isn't
cutting it."

There was concern in Esther's eyes, but she
nodded in agreement. "You need to force
another meeting with Wagner. Our time is
running out with the Cordiers. You need to
discover where they're being held. They're an
important family, and an asset to the Alliance.
Wagner isn't going to be happy about the security breach at the internment camp. I'm sure
he's received the reports by now."

I nodded in agreement. "There is an
urgency to get this done. I feel the few freedoms
we've been allowed these past weeks are dwin-
dling. The restrictions have grown week by
week. I don't know how much longer we can be
operational here."

"George and I feel the same," Esther said.
"Just keep your bag ready. That's why we have
escape plans in place."

The maid brought out my breakfast and I
asked her for stationery so I could have Esther
write the note for me. I didn't write French as
well as I could speak it, and I didn't want to
make any mistakes at this crucial juncture.

"I'll go early in the morning and get my new
cases from Monsieur LeCompte," I said, refer-

ring to the man who owned the makeup company. He was also an Alliance member, which was how I got the job. "I'll head straight to Gestapo headquarters from the office."

I hesitated, wondering if I should mention the fact that Graham had given me a side mission to collect the makeup tin the maid planted inside my case and carry it to another location on my route. And then I wondered if I'd be messing something up by visiting Helene early and off schedule.

I couldn't worry about that now. My priority mission was to discover the location of the Cordier family, and if possible, ascertain if they were still alive.

Esther sealed the envelope with wax and then rang for another servant, handing him the envelope and giving instructions on the delivery. Just as the servant was leaving, another maid walked into the breakfast room with a beautiful bouquet of red roses. There was a note attached.

"Maybe he hasn't gotten the news yet," I said to Esther, looking at the roses as if they were poisonous. "Someone who's just been told that half of his prisoners are gone probably won't be in a flower-sending mood."

"Good point," she said. "Maybe his officers are still trying to decide who should be the bearer of bad news. I wouldn't want that job.

Wagner is known for shooting the messenger. Literally. What does the card say?"

I took the card from the maid and turned over the expensive stationery in my hand. And then I slid my finger under the flap and opened it.

"He wrote it himself," I said, recognizing his handwriting. "He says he'd like to take me on a drive along the coast this afternoon and get to know me better. That I have consumed his thoughts since the moment he laid eyes on me. That definitely doesn't sound like a man who's just been given bad news. But it does fit his profile. Wagner considers himself a romantic, and he wines and dines his conquests lavishly."

"Until he gets tired of them," Esther said warningly.

"Then I just have to make sure he doesn't get tired of me," I said, pushing back from the table. "He's sending a car for me at one o'clock. I'd better go get ready. A soak in the tub sounds like exactly what I need."

"You should probably work on getting that stupid grin off your face too," Esther said. "A man like Wagner is going to recognize that look, and he's going to realize he wasn't the one who gave it to you."

～

I chose my clothing carefully, going with a navy and polka dot dress that nipped in tight at the waist and accentuated my generous bosom. The sleeves were capped and the skirt floated around my knees flirtily. I paired in with a jaunty navy hat with a large white flower on the side and white gloves. I slicked my lips with red and touched my cheeks with rouge. My lashes were thick and dark, so I'd never used mascara.

There was a knock at the door, and I looked at the clock, noticing there was still plenty of time before the car arrived to pick me up.

"Come in," I said, moving to the table where I'd laid my knife, carefully sliding my handbag on top of it so it was concealed.

Margueritte poked her head in the door and said, "Pardon me, *mademoiselle*, but Mr. Smithers would like to see you in his office."

"Thank you, Margueritte," I said. "I'll be right down."

She nodded and closed the door, and I quickly tied the knife to my garter and practiced pulling it a couple of times to make sure it was in a comfortable spot. It was the only thing my father had given me before he'd sent his only daughter across the ocean to live with strangers. In fact, it might have been the only thing he'd ever given me. I couldn't really remember.

I didn't know why I was thinking of my father now, but it wasn't the time. Wild Bill

Holmes had never brought anything but misery to anyone he ever came across, unless they were making him money. Then he could be a real delight. But having him in my thoughts was a distraction, and I couldn't afford any distractions. Wagner wasn't a stupid man, and I knew he was studying me as much as I was studying him.

I'd never been called to George Smithers' study before. I assumed that Esther had told him about my plans for the afternoon and he had specific instructions for me. George was my host, but he was also my direct contact for mission assignments. He'd been in my debriefing along with Graham and two other men who didn't tell me their names.

I knocked on the heavy walnut door and he opened it himself, ushering me inside. George was a big man who carried a slight paunch around his middle. He reminded me of a walrus with his bushy mustache, squinty eyes, and bald head, but his mind was brilliant.

He closed the door behind me and then went directly to the bookcase behind his desk, pulling on a copy of *A Tale of Two Cities*. There was a soft click and the bookcase swung open.

"Come," he said softly, ushering me through the opening and into the dark tunnel. I heard a match light behind me and saw him put flame to wick in an oil lamp, and then he closed the bookcase behind him.

I'd been told the tunnel had been in existence since the Revolution, and those who'd known of its existence were considered the official secret keepers, who had been passed from generation to generation.

There were several different paths to take, and then others that had been blocked with stones. It smelled of earth and the sea, and I was careful not to brush up against anything so as not to muss my clothing.

It was no more than a five-minute walk since the Smitherses lived close to Number 1 Dorset Square. I'd made the trek several times before to the Alliance headquarters, so I knew to watch my step toward the end of the tunnel as it inclined slightly.

George knocked twice on the wall in front of us, waited several seconds, and then knocked four more times at a slightly faster tempo. There was an answering knock from the other side and then George knocked once more. The knock from the other side had been a question of sorts. It was asking if the person on the other side was there of their own free will or if the enemy was with them. One knock in answer meant everything was as it should be. Two knocks meant that all hell would break loose the second the door creaked open.

The door on this side was heavier and made of stone and metal, which made sense since we were walking through a fireplace to get into Number 1 Dorset Square. I blinked my eyes as they adjusted to the light and took in my surroundings quickly.

It was a billiards room, and the walls were done in a burgundy silk and the curtains were a brocade a shade darker. I met Graham's gaze immediately, but I couldn't read anything there, so I moved to the others. Esther was there, along with George, John Armstrong, and Auguste Dubois. No one was smiling.

John Armstrong was a young British man only a few years older than me. He had a smooth baby face and dark puppy dog eyes that made me want to pat him on the head. He never said much, and almost always had his hands in his pockets.

Auguste Dubois looked dangerous. It was the only way to describe him, and I found myself studying his face when he wasn't looking. He was a man of mystery—a Frenchman— short and stocky in his three-piece suit. His hair was dark and his skin swarthy. He was seasoned at the game, that much was obvious, and he seemed impatient to be here. I had a feeling he was busy enough with his own missions, and didn't appreciate getting pulled into ours.

"What's happened?" I asked.

"Wagner had the staff at each of the Gestapo headquarters executed this morning after he received the news of the raid at Vitrolles," Graham said. "Maids, kitchen staff, drivers…most were innocent. We lost seven agents we had working undercover as staff."

I felt my mouth go dry, thinking of Esther's comment about how Wagner had a habit of shooting the messenger when he got bad news, and apparently, everything in his path.

"He suspects someone who had daily contact with them overheard the location of the new internment camp once Les Milles shut down," George said. "The most obvious choice was the staff."

"He's laid their bodies along the avenue as an example," Graham said. "His orders are to let them rot there, and to let the people see what happens to those who betray them."

"And then he sent me two dozen roses and requested I accompany him on a scenic drive," I said, understanding the urgency of this impromptu meeting.

"He's a psychopath," Esther said, her beautiful face rigid with anger and grief. She turned to her husband. "It is too dangerous to send her on this mission. Wagner will start looking for others who have come across his path, who could've shared secrets, and their fates will be like our friends whose blood runs in the streets."

"Settle, my dear," George said, putting his hand on her shoulder gently. It was the first time I'd ever seen him show affection to her, and it was odd, but her body relaxed beneath his touch.

"It is this very reason why I believe Miss Holmes must go through with this charade," he said.

"Can she pull it off?" Auguste Dubois asked, his gaze inspecting me like a horse at auction.

"She can," Graham said confidently. "And at this point, Wagner would be more suspicious if she cancelled their appointment than if she goes through with it." His gaze bored into mine and I felt the tingles down my spine. "I assume you're suitably armed in case something goes wrong?"

"On both accounts," I assured him, referring to my knife and the small white pill in my locket.

He nodded, satisfied, and I guessed that was good enough for the others.

"You have a new mission," George said. "You must get him to take you back to his rooms at some point very soon. We feel after his actions today that the Cordiers have very little time left before they become his next example. One of our last bits of intelligence from Lise before she was killed was that both sets of twins and their father are still alive. Jean Cordier has sensitive information, and all we can do is pray they haven't tortured it from him yet."

"Jean wouldn't betray the Alliance," Auguste said. "He'd die first."

George nodded in agreement, and his stare was intense. "You must be a distraction for Wagner. You must keep him occupied through the night, and it must be within the next two nights. Dr. Meissner took the train to Lambsec as a precaution to make sure there wouldn't be a raid there as well to release prisoners, but we expect him back before the end of the week. Things are chaotic and scattered right now. It's the perfect time to move. To keep Wagner off guard, and to undermine his authority and everything he's trying to build in Marseille. We can take this city back."

"I understand," I said, and my gaze met Graham's. "I need to be going. The car will be here to pick me up soon."

"I'll escort you back," Graham said, taking my arm and leading me back through the secret passageway through the fireplace.

We moved in silence, but I relished the time together with his hand in mine. We hadn't spent any time together outside of formal briefings or my bedroom. I didn't know anything about him, not even where he was staying in Marseille.

"Promise me you'll be careful," he said when we arrived at the back of the bookcase that led to the Smithers' home.

"Always am," I said cheekily.

He took my arm and pulled me toward him, and his face was in shadow. "I mean it," he whispered. "He's insane and volatile. He's just murdered dozens of people in cold blood. People he had no proof betrayed him. They were just possibilities, as are you. He's eliminating loose ends. You are too important to be glib about your safety."

"I'm not naïve enough to think that the Alliance can't replace me if anything should happen."

"*I* can't replace you," he said. "To hell with the Alliance."

I was speechless for a moment, and then I nodded, hoping I understood what he was saying between the lines.

"I'll be careful," I promised.

"If you can't accomplish your task," he said, smoothing his thumb across my cheek. "If you fear things aren't going the way you've planned. Don't take any chances. Slit his throat and get out. You're worth much more alive than dead."

"I'll accomplish the task," I assured him.

"Yes," he said, approvingly. "I believe you will. I can't imagine a man in his right mind ever denying you."

And then he pulled me to him and kissed me like I'd never been kissed before. There was a desperation in his touch I couldn't decipher. But

I wanted more of it. When he pulled us apart, we were both panting for breath.

"Hurry," he said, hitting a hidden switch so the bookcase creaked open. "You have time to fix your lipstick before the car arrives."

CHAPTER 4

I hadn't expected Wagner to be driving the car when it parked in front of the Smithers' home.

I'd been watching from the parlor window, and my eyes had widened when he'd gotten out of the vehicle, dressed smartly in his uniform and cap. He pulled off his leather driving gloves and laid them over the steering wheel and then he came to the door. He didn't look like a man who was ready to kill me.

The bell rang and I inhaled a nervous breath before exhaling slowly. I'd decided the best course of action was to be anxiously awaiting, as if I couldn't stand to be apart from him one more moment.

When the butler answered the door, I made sure Wagner was able to see me immediately.

"My dear," he said, bowing sharply.

"Friedrich," I said, somewhat breathlessly.

"I'm so glad to have received your letter this morning. And the flowers. The flowers are so beautiful. You spoil me so."

"You deserve to be spoiled," he said, kissing my hand. "You look stunning." I blushed prettily and gazed deep into his soulless eyes. "I hope I'm not being too forward, but I thought a drive might be nice. I'd like to spend more time with you. Private time. It's hard for a man in my position to have much privacy. I have to make it when I can."

"I understand," I said. "You're very important. So many people rely on you."

"It's true," he said, taking my hand and tucking it beneath his arm. "I've been working too hard. But seeing you makes me want to pursue other things."

He led me out of the house and down the steps to his car, and I fought the urge to turn back and look at my sanctuary. I thought Graham probably watched me from afar and wondered if I'd ever come back to him. I had to wonder the same thing myself.

I could see the strain on Wagner's face, despite his best effort at joviality. He opened the car door for me and then hurried to the other side, pulling on his gloves and slipping behind the wheel. It wasn't a military vehicle but a beautiful Delahaye in bold navy with silver trim.

The seats were tan leather and the top was down.

"The afternoon belongs to you," he said, starting the engine. "I've taken the liberty of having some cheese and wine packed in the back seat."

"It sounds lovely," I said, scooting subtly closer to him on the seat. I crossed my legs and made sure the hem of my skirt came high enough to show a hint of the top of my stocking. His eyes were immediately drawn there, and then his head snapped up and he swerved to avoid hitting the sidewalk.

"I feel so free with you," I told him boldly. "So comfortable. As if we could just keep driving and sneak away so no one knows where to find us." I lifted my arms in the air and tilted my face toward the sun, knowing it put my body on display. When I looked over at Wagner with laughing eyes, I knew I had him right where I wanted.

"You are too young and innocent to know what you do to me," he admitted.

I blinked several times, looking perplexed. "What do you mean?"

"Not everyone deserves the freedom you crave," he said. "The need to sneak away and escape whatever ails you."

It was then I realized where he was driving us. He'd taken the turn to go down the avenue, and I smelled the blood before I saw the bodies. I gasped in horror and put my hand over my mouth, fighting to keep the anger out of my eyes and make him believe I was new to this kind of revulsion.

"What's happening?" I asked. "I don't understand." I moved closer to him, as if I trusted the monster would save me from himself.

His eyes hardened and he slowed the vehicle, making sure I saw his handywork, and enjoying my reaction more than any sane person should have. But we already knew he was anything but sane.

It was then I wondered if he was showing me my fate. As if he were giving me the opportunity to select where I wanted him to display me.

"Oh, Friedrich," I said, clutching his knee. I needed to get him back on track. Focused on the fantasies and possibilities.

"Pardon me, my dear," he said. "I should have realized you were much too sensitive to see horrors such as this."

"Who…who were they?" I asked, letting a single tear fall prettily from the corner of my eye.

"Traitors," he said simply. "You might even recognize some of them. They worked for me and my officers in one capacity or another. They left me no choice. Traitors must be dealt with harshly, and their bodies send a message to anyone else who has delusions to follow in their footsteps."

He looked at me coldly, and for a split second I wondered if he knew who I was and that I would gladly slit his throat if given the opportunity.

It was only seconds, but the madness passed from his eyes and he pressed harder on the accelerator, leaving the horrors in our rearview.

"Please accept my apologies," he said, taking my hand and kissing my fingers. It was an intimate move, one he hadn't ventured to make as of yet. "I forget how young you are, and I imagine as an American you're not used to the hardships of war like we are here. I'm afraid I'm hardened to such things."

He squeezed my hand and let out a sigh as if the weight of the world had just fallen from his shoulders.

"I could tell when you picked me up something heavy weighed on you," I said, playing to his ego. "Important men like you have important responsibilities. I don't think I could do it."

"Fortunately, you have someone like me so you don't have to," he said.

"That sounds nice," I said, fluttering my lashes instead of rolling my eyes.

The farther we drove down the coast and away from Marseille, the more I prepared myself to fight for my life. I'd had some basic training, but hadn't had a lot of opportunity to put it into practice. Actually, I'd had no opportunities. I'd been successful living in the shadows without suspicion since my inception into the Alliance.

I checked the side mirror occasionally, and inched my way closer to him, checking to see if anyone followed us. But we were alone as far as I could tell. He was taking a chance not having an escort, but maybe he didn't think a woman my size would be much of a threat. Or maybe he had an ambush waiting at our destination.

"Tell me of your family," Wagner said. "Would they approve of me as a contender for your heart?"

"Is that what you are?" I asked, raising a brow and putting my hand back on his knee. "I think I like the sound of that."

I let my fingers stroke in slow circles on his knee while he parked the car on the edge of the road on a curve facing the Gulf of Lion.

"I have a confession to make," I said when he opened my door and helped me out.

"Oh?" he asked. "What kind of confession? Something deep and dark?"

"No, nothing so sinister," I said, laughing gaily. "But it is a bit embarrassing."

"You can trust me," he said. "I hope you know that. We all have secrets that we'd rather keep to ourselves, but it's important we find someone we can trust. Someone who knows the good, the bad, and the ugly."

"You're right," I said, letting my vulnerability show. "I guess I've never had anyone I could trust like that. Not even my family."

"Family is often the hardest to trust and the first to turn on you," he said. "You told me at dinner the other night it wasn't your choice to come here. But you're a dutiful daughter and you came to find a husband like your father wanted. That's very commendable."

"Thank you," I said softly, licking my lips and watching his gaze fall there.

He took a basket and a red checkered blanket from the back seat and laid it flat on a patch of grass. And then he unpacked the basket —square tins of different cheeses and a loaf of fresh bread. There were two wine glasses, and I could see the label on the bottle he uncorked. It was a fine bottle of wine more than a dozen years old, and I wondered where he'd gotten it —or who he'd taken it from. Wine wasn't easy to come by these days.

"Sit, my dear," he said, passing me a glass filled with dark red liquid. "And share your confession."

I inhaled the bouquet. I hated wine. I'd grown up with a taste for whiskey, but I pretended to take a sip and then settled my skirt as I knelt next to him on the blanket.

"Well then, if I'm going to confess then you must know I sent a note to Helene today. I saw in the paper the train was coming in from Paris with supplies, and coming by to see Helene was the only thing I could think of so I could see you sooner. I was afraid you wouldn't call on me again."

His face creased into a smile and he took my wine glass from me, setting them both aside. "I think that's wonderful," he said. "I have a confession to make too."

He'd moved subtly closer and I knew he was going to try and kiss me. I pretended it was Graham in front of me, and I looked at Wagner with nothing but love and desire.

"Tell me," I whispered.

"I'm finding it very hard to act like a gentleman around you," he said. I felt his breath against my lips and then he nipped at my bottom lip. "I don't think you realize how beautiful you are. How enticing to a man's senses. I want you very much. Do you know what I mean by that?"

I nodded and said, "I think so." And then I bit my lip in worry. "Are you asking me to be your lover?"

"I am," he said. "I'd also like you to be my

wife. But right now I need to be alone with you."

"We're alone now," I said breathlessly.

"No," he said, shaking his head. "I'm never alone. There's always someone watching."

I frowned at that. How had I not seen or felt eyes on us?

"Don't worry," he said, smoothing the lines from my face. "They won't bother us. And they're very discreet. After the events of last night and this morning it's best to take extra precautions."

"What happened last night?" I asked.

His expression darkened. "I don't want to ruin the moment by discussing it, and it's nothing for you to worry about. What I'm asking is if you're willing to come to me tomorrow night. We'll have the house to ourselves, and I'll plan a romantic dinner. In essence, we'll have our honeymoon before the wedding."

"Yes," I burst out, my excitement barely contained. From what I gathered, he seemed to enjoy the fact that I was innocent and naïve. I could sense the evil in him, the innate need to destroy, whether it was the people of Marseille or my innocence. Maybe there were some men who wanted to cherish and protect their women, but I had yet to meet one, so I wasn't surprised.

"I want to be with you too," I told him. "Are

you sure no one would know? I'd hate for my friends to discover my indiscretions. My reputation is important to me."

"I'd never do anything to harm your reputation," he said. "I've sent Helene and the other women to different areas. Their work called for something else. And the two guards I'll have will stay on the first floor, but I can assure you they will be completely discreet or they'll answer to me. I wouldn't want to leave either of us unprotected for the night. These are unsafe times."

I swallowed nervously. "Okay," I said. "I'd be lying if I said I wasn't hesitant. I've never known a man like you. You're so sophisticated and worldly. So romantic. You've swept me off my feet, and things are moving so fast. But these feelings I have for you. I can't deny them." I felt the heat in my cheeks and I lowered my gaze.

"What is it?" he asked.

"I've never had this yearning before. This heat in my body. It's all so new."

Bingo, I thought when I saw the look of triumph in his eyes.

"I'll be gentle," he promised. "And after tomorrow I'll be at your mercy forever."

"I'm counting on it," I said.

CHAPTER 5

I didn't sleep that night.

Partly because of Graham. He continued to come to me during the night, and it felt like he'd always been in my life and in my bed. I'd heard sayings about relationships that burned hot and fast and that they eventually fizzled, but I'd never known anything else. It was the hot and fast that made life interesting. But with Graham, there was part of me that could imagine feeling his weight on the other side of the bed night after night. But I was hesitant to let myself get too hopeful.

I knew my relationship with James Walker had been wrong, but he'd made me feel... special. He gave me attention and doted on me and showered me with gifts. He hung on to my every word like it was the best thing he'd ever heard. And our flame had burned so hot and fast I hadn't stopped to think what we might be lighting on fire along the way.

I'd had interest from men from the time I'd grown breasts, and I'd learned to flirt and pretend I was interested and impressed by what I saw in the opposite sex. My mother had been an excellent teacher in that regard. I'd perfected my techniques until I'd found a man who caught my fancy—a man who knew a thing or two—not a boy who'd be fumbling around like a fool. I'd enjoyed feeling special—even as short-lived as it had been—because I'd realized up to that point that I'd never felt special. And worse, I'd never believed I was special.

Growing up in Whiskey Bayou had been hard. Everything was lacking—from supplies to education—and I guessed I'd been lucky that I had a natural aptitude for numbers, otherwise I wouldn't have spent a lick of time in a school-room or with tutors like most of the other girls my age. That had been the only thing I could think of that my father had done right. And even that, he'd done for his own benefit. I made him money, so I was worth something to him.

When James Walker had come along, he'd made the other men I'd let catch my eye seem like amateurs. But he'd ultimately been my destruction, and he hadn't even bothered to say goodbye when I'd been so hastily put on the first ship to France.

I wasn't sure I'd ever be able to feel anything for a man after James. He'd broken my heart, and I'd vowed to never give that much of myself to another man again. But where James had been smooth talk and cool sophistication, Henry Graham was rough and tumble and unpolished. His brain worked at a speed I felt matched my own and he was quick-witted and sharp-tongued. While James had fawned over me and treated me as something delicate, Graham treated me as an equal. It was an entirely different feeling. And my feelings for him were entirely different than they'd been for James.

We hadn't known each other but for days, yet I felt as if I'd known him forever. There was a connection that penetrated the soul, and it was terrifying and exhilarating all at once. I couldn't help but wonder how he felt about my mission. Did he worry for my safety? Was he jealous that I had to play the seductress to lure the enemy?

Graham was only part of the reason I hadn't slept. He'd slipped out sometime during the night like usual, but dreams had plagued me of the bodies I'd seen on the street. I had recognized some of the gray faces whose empty eyes had stared blankly at a cerulean sky.

I thought endlessly about my upcoming task and what I had to do, and I shut off the part of my brain that hated the fact that my body and my looks continued to have more of a purpose in my life than my brains. If I didn't know any better, I'd have said I felt shame. But that was ridiculous because Holmeses weren't ashamed of anything. Holmeses fought and scrapped and climbed their way to whatever they wanted, and they had no regrets on how they got there.

I finally gave up on sleep and decided to get up and get dressed for the day. We were to meet at Number 1 Dorset Square at eight o'clock sharp. Nerves fluttered like butterflies in my stomach as I went about washing up and getting dressed. I'd be primped and pampered and perfumed before I left for my mission at Gestapo headquarters.

For now, I donned a pair of high-waisted pale gray pants and a blousy navy shirt I wore tucked in. I rolled up the sleeves and then wrapped a kerchief in my hair, tying it in a knot on top of my head. I'd brushed out my curls until they'd crackled and rubbed a small amount of perfume between my hands before smoothing them over my hair. It tamed the frizzies and calmed the curls. I slipped on my oxfords and made my way to the kitchen.

I knew the staff would be up and preparing to start their day, but I figured the Smitherses and anyone else who might have been in residence would be asleep a while longer. I crept down from the third floor using the old servant stairs that led directly to the kitchen. I figured coffee and toast would settle my stomach, and if that failed I knew where George kept his bottle of whiskey in his office. In my experience, whiskey cured most things.

I could hear whispers and something heavy banging from the kitchen, but when I walked in, a pregnant silence filled the room. The only thing I cared about was the smell of freshly pressed coffee that permeated air.

All of the staff in the Smithers' home had come with them from London, and only those who were the most trusted. Servants made as good of spies as anyone in the Alliance, which was why Lise and her friends were rotting in the street.

"I don't mean to intrude," I said in English. "I'll help myself to coffee and slip out."

"I'll get it, ma'am," Mrs. Worth said, laying down her rolling pin and the fresh dough she was working over.

She set it up on a small tray with cream and sugar, and added dry toasts and crockeries of butter and jam. She added a pastry, and I started to think maybe I could eat after all.

"Are you eating in the dining room?" she asked.

I nodded, because it was very obvious taking a seat at the kitchen table wouldn't have been welcome. I preceded her into the dining room and took my place so I could see out the front windows that looked out along the pier. They were the same boats that had been docked the day before and the day before that.

You could feel something brewing in the air, as if everything was ripping apart at the seams. The only thing any of us could do was keep putting one foot in front of the other until we stepped on a land mine.

I felt his presence before I saw or heard him, and then I felt his hand squeeze the back of my neck as he bent down to kiss the top of my head.

"I didn't expect to see you today," I said. "I can ring for more coffee."

"I came in through the kitchen like you," he said, smiling as he took the seat at the head of the table facing the door and the windows. Graham never put himself in a position to be taken by surprise. "It drives Mrs. Worth crazy to have people in her space."

There was a boyish charm as he spoke of Mrs. Worth. "And how long have you been aggravating her?" I asked.

"Oh, about a decade or so," he said. "Before George and Esther were married. Mrs. Worth was George's family's cook when he was a boy."

I was like a sponge for information about him. "How long have you known George?"

"He was my recruiter at MI6," he said.

"George?" I asked. "I didn't realize."

"Marriage changes a man," Graham said.

"The George you see now is not the George I knew at the beginning of my career. And still, I wouldn't want to go up against him one-on-one. But he withdrew from the more dangerous jobs after he and Esther married, and then he recruited her as well, so a lot of their undercover work is as a married couple and in society."

"How did you end up in France?" I asked.

"I guess I'm a bit of a rogue at heart," he said, grinning. "I tend to end up where I'm needed. I've lived here and there and everywhere. Nothing has stuck permanently. But when George mentioned that MI6 was creating the Special Operations Executive, and he was to head up the Alliance out of Marseille, I knew I could be of use to help end this war. I was asked to be in charge of Alliance headquarters in Lyon, but I don't like being in charge. Being in charge means you have to sit behind a desk instead of breaking into prisons in the middle of the night."

"Or Gestapo headquarters," I added.

"Exactly," he said.

I hesitated, wanting to ask more, but I took a sip of coffee instead.

"What is it?" he asked.

"No one has talked about what happens after," I said. "What happens if we're all successful in our missions? What happens when the Cordiers are rescued and exported out of the city? What happens when Wagner wakes up in the morning with a terrible hangover and a realization he's been duped? He's going to go on a rampage through this city like nothing these people have ever seen."

"Hitler will call him ineffective and demote him," Graham said. "He'll be scrubbing toilets back in Germany before the week is out."

I wanted to believe that, but I wasn't so sure. Men like Wagner didn't disappear so easily once they'd had a taste of power.

"All things considered," he said. "This is a simple, straightforward job. You've played your part beautifully. We've been getting briefings and intelligence reports on Meissner and his comings and goings, as well as how Wagner is positioning his officers around the city. He's moved the women out of head-quarters and into one of the other houses they've commandeered. Don't underestimate Helene. She'll be more of a threat to us after this mission than Wagner will. Those women are a group of finely trained machines. All of the work that's been accomplished since Wagner took over the city is because of her strategies and investigative work."

I didn't know how to put into words what I was feeling. This was a job. This wasn't real life. We were all living lies to the point that the truth was becoming more and more difficult to decipher.

"Ah," Graham said, taking my hand. "You're thinking when your mission is complete that you'll be displaced."

"It's not like I can keep peddling makeup after today," I said. "At least, not unless I want a bullet in my head."

"That would be a travesty," he said. "Your brain is one of my favorite things about you."

Heat rushed to my face.

"You're not comfortable with compliments," he said. "I wonder why."

"Of course I am," I said, hating that he saw through me that easily.

"You're comfortable with compliments about your looks. I bet you get told you're beautiful a hundred times a day. And you are. You're probably the most beautiful woman I've ever seen. But I've watched you, and I've heard George sing your praises for weeks. You not only have a photographic memory, but you've been able to dictate conversations you've had and overheard in their entirety. You've picked up languages and learned skills it sometimes takes new trainees months to a year to learn."

It was a challenge to keep from squirming in my seat at his assessment of me, and I wondered if he was doing it on purpose just to see if he could make me squirm.

"What are you getting at?" I asked.

"I'm saying that after this mission is done, you're going to have your pick of what's next. And if America ever decides to join this fight, I predict there's going to be an interesting negotiation over your services between MI6 and the OSS."

"And what about you?" I asked, pretending I was braver than I was. I didn't really want to hear his answer, but I had to ask. "Where will you be?"

"I'll be like you," he said. "Wherever they send me. Which according to the letter I received yesterday is Belgium. I'll take the command position at the new Alliance headquarters there. And you'll start a new cover under my command. If you'd like to accept the job."

I arched a brow and my mouth tilted up at the corner. "And what about during the night?"

He picked up my hand and brought it to his mouth, his eyes telling me everything I wanted to know. "During the night, you get to be in charge."

"Then it looks like we're going to Belgium."

CHAPTER 6

An hour later I was at Number 1 Dorset Square, standing over the blueprints of the Schwartz house.

George and Esther were with me, along with Graham, Auguste, and John Armstrong. The team was small, but they insisted it was all the manpower that was needed to take their headquarters and free the Cordiers.

"Wagner made it a point to tell me that only two of his officers would be on site," I said. "And that they'd be contained to the first floor so we'd have complete privacy."

"The first floor has the large entry area you've seen before," George said. "There's a front parlor…"

"That's completely empty," Graham said. "I had a good view in there after Scarlet ran me down."

"I still don't know how you ended up in front of my car," I said.

"That's easy," Graham said. "Because you're a terrible driver."

"Moving on," George said. "The kitchen is also on the first floor and takes up almost the entire back half. There's a front stairway…"

"Which is the one I've taken each week to meet Helene and the other women on the fourth floor."

"But there's also a secondary staircase in the back leading up from the kitchen," George finished. "I've got a rough sketch diagram from what information Lise was able to give me."

"You'd think she'd have been able to pinpoint the Cordiers' location inside the house," I said. "Servants observe and know everything."

"That's the thing," Graham said. "There was a basic skeleton crew of domestic staff. Lise, another girl, and a cook. None of them were live-ins. And they were all given strict instructions on what they could and could not do, and where they could and could not go. The second floor was completely off limits, but so were the servant stairs. We have good intel on all of the other areas."

"Dr. Meissner allowed people into his personal space?" I asked, surprised, remembering Meissner was on the third floor.

"Yes," Graham said. "Meissner is known for having some interesting quirks along with just being insane."

"As if that isn't enough," I said.

"He's very particular about his living and work spaces," George said. "He has an aversion to anything dirty. He's been known to wash his hands to the point his skin gets raw."

"Considering some of the horrible things he does with those hands, I'm not surprised," I said.

"He's just as particular about his rooms," Graham said. "No dust, no papers out of order, no empty coffee cups, and no smudges. He insists that bleach be used to wipe down all the surfaces in the areas he occupies.

"I feel like I need to be worried about what I'm going to be walking into tonight if Wagner hasn't had his rooms cleaned in weeks. It's hard to be seductive with dirty underpants on the floor and cobwebs hanging from the ceiling."

Graham coughed to cover a laugh, though his eyes were sparkling. "I'm sure you'll figure out a way to make it work. Besides, I was up there a few days ago and everything looked clean and in its place. And there were no underpants on the floor."

"Good to know," I said. "I'm assuming you got a good look at what I'm about to walk into?"

"He's got the whole second floor to himself,"

Graham said. "It must have been the floor where the children and their nanny stayed, because it's a large open space and the wallpaper is softer in color. But everything has been stripped out and all of Wagner's personal belongings are there.

"The floor is split into two areas once you come off the landing from the stairs," he continued. "His sleeping quarters are on the left and his office on the right. The office area is set up for meetings with his command staff, and he has maps laid out with troops and positions.

"They didn't let me get close enough to the map to get a good look at it. They put me on a little sofa right off the stairs and I waited until Meissner came to see me. There's nothing much to be done for scrapes and bruises, and they didn't get any important information by questioning me. Part of my cover is my connections to very wealthy Nazi sympathizers. Wagner would have had to hold me for too long while he checked my cover story, so he took me at my word and released me."

The blueprints didn't tell me a lot about what I'd be walking into tonight. It showed me the structure, which was helpful, but it told me nothing about Wagner. Which Wagner would I meet tonight? The romantic gentleman who sent flowers? Or the crazed madman who wanted to see my reaction to the deaths he'd caused?

"I've been to the fourth floor extensively when I met with Helene and the other women," I said. "There's no place the Cordiers could be hiding there. There are no other rooms on these blueprints. Someone has been to every area."

"Except for the servant stairs," Graham said. "Homes like these typically have false walls or hidden rooms that wouldn't be in the plans."

"It could take hours to find a hidden room in that house," I said.

"Which is why it's important you keep Wagner busy long enough to do a thorough search," George said.

I avoided Graham's gaze because I hadn't gotten around to asking him if my mission bothered him. I could seduce a man. I could do whatever I needed to do to save the innocent. But I was torn between becoming the spy I'd been born to be, and losing my chance to have the kind of relationship I'd never had. I thought my choices seemed heavy for a seventeen-year-old woman who'd never quite fit in wherever she was.

"I've got it," I said. When I looked up, I caught Esther's eye, and I could see the worry there before she quickly masked her expression.

"I think it's time to get you ready," Esther

said, coming forward and taking me by the arm. "Presentation is going to be important tonight. Appearances are important to Wagner, as important as setting the scene correctly."

I let my gaze meet that of each of the men, letting them know I wasn't afraid to do my job and that they could count on me. I had the power to do something none of them could accomplish, and I needed to remember that. Auguste and John Armstrong both gave me a respectful nod. And George, bless his stiff-necked heart, tried to smile, but only managed to move his mustache slightly off-kilter.

And then I turned to Graham and arched a brow, hiding my feelings behind a cocky grin. He held out a hand and I put mine in his, and he shook it firmly as if I was just one of the guys. And then he jerked me forward and planted a kiss on my lips that had the others hooting with laughter.

"Don't get killed," he said. "And don't ever relax your guard. Men like Wagner can smell weakness, and he'll go in for the kill."

I nodded and followed Esther through the fireplace and into the secret tunnel that led back to her home.

She laughed when the door closed behind us. "I've heard that Henry Graham's kisses are legendary, but to see the look on your face I have to wonder what I've been missing all these years. I can tell you no man has ever put that look on my face before. You've got to pace yourself. You're young, so you don't want him to ruin men for you for the rest of your life. You'll always be searching for that feeling that doesn't quite live up to what Graham gave you."

I didn't tell her that Graham and I would be heading to Belgium on our next mission, and that if I had my way, we'd be partners in every part of life before we were done. Considering Graham had just gotten his appointment to take command at the Alliance headquarters in Belgium, I wanted to safeguard his secret until he was ready to tell the others.

Formal dinners were much later in the evening than I was used to back home, and it's not like I'd be able to eat anyway on a nervous stomach. But Wagner had sent another bouquet of flowers with a note telling me to dress in my finest for dinner and that he was sending a car to pick me up at nine o'clock.

French couture clothing wasn't as easy to come by as it had been even a few months ago, but Esther knew a seamstress who'd lost her shop when Paris had been bombed the week before and she'd escaped with not much more than the clothes on her back and come to stay with her family in Marseille.

Esther led me to her personal quarters. They were lush and opulent, and I wasn't even able to open my mouth in protest in time to stop the maids from stripping me down to nothing and scrubbing me within an inch of my life. I was shaved and perfumed, and my hair was curled and piled stylishly on top of my head.

I was wrapped in a soft silk robe and placed in a chair, and then cream was slathered on my face before they darkened and smudged my eyelids and painted my lips the color of rubies.

"Stunning," Esther said, clapping her hands together excitedly. "Absolutely stunning. If he's able to form a sentence I'd be surprised. This should be the easiest job you've ever had."

A small, birdlike woman walked into the room at that moment with dress bags over her arm. Her hair was jet black and pulled back from a pointed face with a hawkish nose. She wasn't an attractive woman, but she commanded the room.

"Stand," she said in crisp French. "Take off your robe and stand over here."

"Scarlet," Esther said. "This is Madame Blanche. You are very lucky to be wearing one of her creations."

Seconds later, I found myself standing on a small platform completely naked. She opened the dress bag and pulled out a long column of scarlet, and I was mesmerized by the richness of the color.

It was simple in design until I stepped into the column and she brought it to my waist, tucking and pinning as she went. Two swathes of silk hung down in front of me and she pulled them up, arranging the silk over one shoulder, tucking only one of my breasts behind the opaque fabric.

Esther sighed. "I've dreamed of having a body like yours. The damage I could do to the male population with breasts like those."

My lips twitched. "Is this the new style?" I asked. "To leave one breast completely exposed? I've heard stories of the French, of course, but this seems like it might be asking for trouble in a drive all the way across town."

Esther laughed, and Madame Blanche swatted my hands away and clucked her tongue as if dressing me was beneath her. To be honest, it probably was beneath her. Clothes like these were completely wasted on me. I'd much rather something comfortable that I could move quickly and freely if I got in an interesting situation.

Madame Blanche had a needle and thread in her mouth, and she held an embroidered strip of sheer cloth in the same vibrant red. She tucked and stitched the piece and then brought it up over my bare breast, attaching it at my shoulder where the other fabric met.

"Oh, my," Esther said. "Just lovely."

When I turned to look at myself in the mirror I didn't recognize the woman standing there. It certainly didn't look like the girl from Whiskey Bayou I'd once known.

The shade of red she'd chosen complemented my skin. My eyes were smudged at the corners and my lashes full and long. And that one scrap of sheer material with the embroidery made a simple dress exceptional. A flower had been sewn strategically into the fabric and kept the dress from being indecent. Just barely.

Madame Blanche knelt at my feet and sewed the hem of the dress so it stopped at the tip of my shoes. And then she stood up and stuck her various pins and needles back in the pincushion, gathered her things, and looked at Esther expectantly.

"Thank you, Madame Blanche," Esther said. "This is exceptional work on such short notice. It's close to curfew. You're welcome to stay in our guest suite."

"I have time to make it home," she said. "My driver is still sitting out front."

Esther nodded, and without a goodbye, the tiny woman walked out of the room.

"How do you feel?" Esther asked once we were alone.

"Like I hate to waste this dress on someone like Friedrich Wagner," I said. "I feel like Graham would be much more appreciative. I supposed I shouldn't worry that Madame Blanche didn't give me any underthings to put on."

Esther smiled. "A dress like this is not meant for underthings."

"That's what I thought," I said, holding the skirt and swishing it back and forth. "It has good movement. But I don't have a place for my knife."

I couldn't remember the last time I'd gone anywhere without it, and I stepped off the platform and went to my trousers the maid had folded and put on the dresser. I felt in the pocket and pulled out the leather sheath and the sharp blade. It was a security blanket of sorts, the only sentimental thing I'd brought with me from home.

"Yes, that will definitely leave a line in a dress like this," Esther said. "The skirt is somewhat transparent in the light as you walk. You'll have to keep it in your handbag. Go ahead and tie it to a garter so you can slip it on if you need to move quickly."

"Good thinking," I said, giving her the knife. Neither of us mentioned that my hands shook slightly as she took the knife from me.

"I'm not used to going into a situation like

this unprotected," I said. "Between the sheerness of the dress and my knife not readily available, it makes me very vulnerable to Wagner. He could overpower me in a moment and that would be that."

"But he won't, because you'll be so convincingly seductive that he'll be a puddle at your feet," she said. "Something I've learned over the years is the faster you can get a man naked the less suspicious they become of you. They can only think with one brain at a time. But just in case, I think I have the perfect finishing touch for you."

"What is it?" I asked, watching her take a locked leather case from the bed.

"Sometimes women need a little ingenuity for safety reasons," she said, smiling. "This should do nicely."

Esther unlocked the case and opened the center compartment, and then opened the two side compartments so the entire case was displayed. "Goodness," I said, eyeing the ruby-and-diamond-encrusted hairpin. It was long and thin like a chopstick, and Esther pulled at the cluster of jewels and it detached from a small scabbard, revealing an ice-thin pick.

"Good for a sneak attack," Esther said. "Especially if you find yourself trapped beneath someone you don't want to be under. A quick stab in the kidneys usually gets them to move off you pretty fast."

"I can imagine," I said, watching her place the hairpin back in the scabbard. Then she slid it carefully into my elaborately coiffed hair.

"Perfect," she said. "Now for the finishing touch." She held up a gold tube and then opened it, twisting the bottom so red lipstick appeared. "You can use it. It matches the lipstick you're wearing now."

Esther put the lid back on and then turned the tube over. She pressed it with her thumb and the bottom cap came off, revealing a small set of silver lock picks. "You never know when you'll need to pick a lock."

"And a great color," I said, placing the lipstick in my handbag along with my knife. I took my heart-shaped locket from on top of my pile of clothes and fastened it around my neck. It was a small silver heart and the chain was short and thin, so it rested at the hollow of my throat. It wasn't as fancy as other jewelry I could've worn to accentuate the dress, but it was dainty and feminine and didn't detract from it either. Besides, I never left home without it.

"You have everything you need," Esther said. "But never forget the best tool you have is right here." She touched her finger to my temple. "All you have to do is get through the night. Tomorrow will be a whole new world."

I nodded and looked at myself again in the mirror, straightening my shoulders. "Dressing to kill is going to have a whole new meaning after this experience."

CHAPTER 7

The driver appeared in front of the Smithers' home at exactly nine o'clock, and I waited patiently as the driver came to collect me. A white fur stole completed my attire, and I clasped my lethal handbag and followed the driver to the car.

The drive didn't take as long as I'd have liked it to, but it was well past curfew and the normally busy streets of Marseille were empty. There was a light summer breeze from the gulf and the smell of the sea ushered me to the front door of what had once been the Schwartz residence.

I tried not to think of Graham and how it had only been a few short days since I'd hit him with my car at this very spot. The driver escorted me up the walk and up the stairs, and the door opened before I could get there.

It was the first time I'd seen Wagner out of uniform, and I had to admit it would be easier to do my job without staring at the repulsive insignia on his arm. He wore a traditional tuxedo, and his hair was combed back from his face and his mustache trimmed.

"My God," he said, his mouth dropping open slightly. "I'm not sure this world is meant to hold beauty like yours."

I beamed at him and moved away from the driver, navigating the stairs myself so I could meet Wagner halfway. "Oh, don't you look handsome." I placed my hands on his chest in an intimate gesture and let him kiss me softly.

"Thank you, driver," he said. "That will be all."

The driver clicked his heels together sharply and saluted, "Heil Hitler," he said, and Wagner repeated the gesture.

I kept the smile on my face even as my skin crawled, and Wagner led me into the house and closed the doors behind us. As he'd said, there were two guards in the front entryway of the home, both at attention, neither of them looking in my direction. It was as if I weren't there at all.

"Absolute discretion," he assured me, putting his hand to the small of my back and leading me toward the stairs.

I knew those two officers would be dead come morning, and I tried not to think about

Graham, Auguste, and John Armstrong breaking into the house without being detected.

"Don't they get tired of standing?" I whispered innocently. "It must be terribly hard to be an officer."

Wagner chuckled condescendingly. "They don't always stand still," he said. "They walk the property and check the entrances to make sure no one is around who shouldn't be. It's a very important job."

"I can imagine," I said. "You must trust them very much if they're your personal guards."

He nodded and followed closely behind me on the stairs, trailing his fingers along the bare part of my back.

"Considering my recent staffing problems," he said. "I took the liberty of procuring the services of Jacque Allard. I brought him in from Paris this morning after you agreed to be my guest. He set everything up beautifully so we can serve ourselves. We'll have no prying eyes and ears tonight. It's just you and me."

"I'd like that very much," I said, ducking my head slightly so he could see my nerves.

When we reached the second-floor landing the space opened up just as Graham had said. I was surprised to see how homey the room was. Wagner had used his time in Marseille to move in more than a few of his personal things. The walls had been freshly painted and rugs put on the floors. The furniture was heavily ornate and dark.

Bookcases filled with books lined the walls, and my eyes were immediately drawn to the large table and the maps that sat upon it. Small figurines and pins dotted the maps, but I let my gaze move over them to the rest of the space. There was a desk and a pair of swords crossed and attached to the wall behind it.

"I'm afraid I spend too much time in my office," he said. "I'll confess, I've even fallen asleep at my desk a time or two."

I looked at him coyly from beneath my lashes. "Well, maybe I can keep you from working tonight."

"A man needs to take a night off every now and again."

My smile spread and I looked at him boldly. "I said I'd keep you from working. But I'm also going to keep you from sleeping."

He inhaled sharply through his nose and I turned away from him and headed toward the smell of food. It was my turn to gasp. There were candles everywhere. And in the middle of the room was a large bed that had been turned down. He'd even gone so far as to sprinkle rose petals on the sheets.

"It's beautiful," I said, touching his hand, and he took my wrap from my shoulders.

When I turned back to face him, I was bathed in the candlelight and I could see Wagner's expression clearly. Madame Blanche was worth her weight in gold. And my only regret was that it wasn't Graham who was looking at me like a blind man seeing for the first time.

Wagner put his hand to his chest.

"Are you all right?" I asked, moving toward him.

"I'm fine, I'm fine," he said. "I just wanted to check and see if my heart was still beating. The sight of you takes my breath away."

"Flattery will get you everything," I said seductively.

"I had a gift for you," he said.

"Had?" I questioned.

He nodded to a long box tied with a red ribbon that sat in an armchair against the wall. "I'm afraid it's a useless gift."

"I love gifts," I said. "Especially when they're useless." I made my way to the chair and picked up the box, slipping off the ribbon so I could lift the lid. Delicate tissue paper lined the box, and underneath it was a sheer black negligee that would've had Madame Blanche blushing.

"I was thinking I'd like for you to slip into this before dinner, but I've changed my mind," he said. "You're perfect as you are. Are you hungry?"

"Starving," I said, giving him a coy smile

and then moving around his personal space, inspecting the smattering of pictures he had sitting on top of his dresser.

He'd made himself quite at home in someone else's house, and it reminded me that he wasn't a man to underestimate. He didn't have a conscience, and there was no reasoning with the Devil.

"Is this your family?" I asked, watching him move to the sideboard and pour two glasses of wine.

"Yes," he said, shooting me a sheepish grin over his shoulder. "I'm afraid you'll find me quite sentimental when it comes to family loyalty."

"I think that's a good thing," I said. "Do you ever think about having a family of your own?"

"My career has always taken precedence when it comes to my priorities in life, but lately I've found myself wanting something different. Something more. I believe that's why we're here tonight."

I laughed, a tinkling sound I'd perfected over the years—one I found men thought quite amusing. "Let's not get too far ahead of ourselves," I admonished. "I believe there's a proper order for weddings and babies." And then I added conspiratorially, "Honeymoons are negotiable, of course."

"Of course," he said, walking toward me

with the wine. He handed me the glass and then he touched his glass to mine. "To a lifetime of honeymoons," he said, gazing deep into my eyes.

"Thank you for making tonight so special," I said, letting him lead me to the table he had set for dinner.

The courses were already laid out, and there were several wine pairings to go with each course. The sight of all that wine and food would have been enough for the people of Marseille to storm the castle, so to speak. They'd been living on rations and scraps for weeks, and I felt guilty for even being in the same room with such waste.

"You have no idea how much I want to skip dinner right now," he said, pulling out my chair.

I sat, somewhat surprised and eternally grateful for his restraint. "We can always move straight to the dessert course."

"Patience, my love," he said. "You deserve the romance and the rituals. Let me wine and dine you. I want us to know all about each other in every way before the night is through."

"Oh, well," I said. "I wish I'd led as exciting of a life as you have."

"You're young yet," he said. "Give yourself time, and you'll have had as many grand adventures as I have. Now let's eat before it gets cold."

I picked at each course, enraptured by his

every word. He told me of his childhood and bragged about how he'd impressed Hitler from their first meeting, and then his rapid rise through the ranks as a commander of an elite police force. He never flinched at the stories he told, or the brutalization of human life. To him, the people he tortured were no more than animals.

The duck in front of me sat cold as I moved the meat around on the plate, waiting for my stomach to settle as he told a particularly gruesome tale of his last visit to Les Milles.

"Is something wrong with the food?" he asked. "You're not eating."

"It's delicious," I told him. "I think the anticipation of tonight has made me a little nervous."

"I'd be lying if I didn't feel the same," he said.

"Can I get you more wine?" I asked, standing to my feet and moving toward the sideboard.

I was thankful that I'd grown up with a father who'd never minded strong spirits in the house. Because if I'd been a normal woman, I would have already been passed out from the different wines we'd had with each course.

"More wine would be wonderful," he said, leaning back in his chair. He was watching me as I moved across the room, and it wasn't an

altogether pleasant look in his eyes. "You're a
very intriguing woman."

"Thank you," I said.

"It feels as if you find that more of a compli-
ment than when I tell you you're beautiful."

"Beauty fades over time," I said. "But I can
be intriguing until my last days on earth."

"I suppose," he said, his frown thoughtful.
"And do you enjoy living a life of intrigue?"

There was something about the tone of his
voice that had me pausing as I stood in front of
the sideboard, studying the final bottle of
unopened wine on the sidebar.

"Like I told you before," I said, "I haven't
lived such an interesting life as of yet."

"Hmm," he said. "Something tells me that
might not be altogether true."

I picked up the wine bottle with surprisingly
steady hands. Something had shifted in the
atmosphere, and I wasn't sure what it was. But I
no longer felt in control of the situation. I no
longer felt like I was the one playing the tune for
him to dance to.

"I don't know what you mean," I said, giving
him a curious look over my shoulder. "Maybe
we've had too much wine." I started to put the
bottle back.

"No, let's finish our meal. I'll have a final
glass."

I expertly uncorked the bottle and smelled it,

inhaling a sweet scent that was sure to be bitter on my tongue.

"Did you really think that I don't have my finger on every pulse in this city?" he asked. "That I'm not aware of every whisper and hushed plan to try and take back this city?" His voice had gone hard and cold, and I'd never heard him speak to me like that before.

It made me realize that our drive by the corpses on the Quai des Belges was for a purpose. He'd been aware of who I was, maybe all along, and I'd become just another pawn in his repertoire of sick games.

"Friedrich," I said. "Are you all right? Maybe dinner isn't settling well. You're not making any sense." I poured the first glass of wine, watching the honey-colored liquid fill the glass.

"Aren't I?" he asked. "This city is mine. There is no one you can trust who is not loyal to me. But you're very good. Better than others who have tried before you."

I rested my hand on the sideboard so he couldn't see it shaking, and I propped a hand on my hip as I squared off with him. Graham's words rattled around in my mind about never showing weakness, so I plastered a cocky grin on my face and figured all I could do at this point was try to brazen my way through.

"Honey," I said. "I don't know what you had

for dinner, but I think it might have been different than mine. You're not making any sense. Come on, now. Stop playing with me. You're starting to hurt my feelings, and I was getting so warm and fuzzy inside."

I turned back to the sideboard and touched the clasp of the locket at my throat, opening the tiny mechanism so a small white pill fell into my hand. I crushed it between my fingers and dropped it into the already poured glass of wine. And then I quickly poured wine into the remaining glass.

My hands were steady as I picked them both up and made my way back to the table. "Here," I told him, handing him the glass. "Let's have dessert and then I'd very much like to try on my present. You have an eye for beautiful things."

"It's always been my biggest weakness," he said, staring at me out of cold blue eyes.

I moved back to the other side of the table and took my seat as if I hadn't a care in the world, all the while praying for a miracle. "Now eat your dessert and tell me a story of another of your adventures," I said.

"I have enjoyed your company," he said, as if I hadn't spoken. "It's a shame, really. You're so young and beautiful, and really quite skilled. But you're new to this world, and it shows. I have eyes and ears everywhere. And I know everything about you, from what you have for breakfast to who shares your bed."

I felt the blood drain from my face, and I thought of every person who'd had a presence in the Smithers' household, from the servants to Esther and George. Someone had betrayed the Alliance.

"Your weakness is that you crave family and friends," he said. "But you haven't learned the most important life lesson of all—the only person you can trust in this world is yourself."

He picked up the wine glass and held it up to the flickering candle, so the light played tricks in the liquid gold.

"It's a shame, really," he said. "I would have liked to have taken you to bed before I killed you, but I find I just don't have the stomach for some things."

He scraped his chair back from the table and got to his feet, and my eyes widened as I considered my options. My handbag was too far away to be of any use, and he was too big and strong for me to fight head-on, even though I'd learned some very effective techniques in my training.

I pushed my own chair back, deciding I had no choice but to fight for my life, and then my miracle happened. He downed the glass of wine in one gulp and then slammed the crystal down on the table, shattering the stem.

He took a step toward me, and then another,

and then his eyes widened and white spittle gathered at the corners of his mouth. He tried to take another step but fell to his knees. And then his eyes met mine and glazed as he gasped his last breath and fell face-first onto the floor.

I wasn't sure how long I sat there, stunned by what had just happened. But I knew it definitely wasn't part of the plan, and the others' lives were in danger. If Wagner knew of my involvement, then he'd surely trusted his officers with the same information. I had to get word to Graham, though I feared it was too late.

It was almost midnight, and if they weren't already inside the house, they were attempting to breach its doors. Only to walk right into a trap.

My mission was my failure, but the Cordiers were counting on Graham and his team to be a success. I had to help them however I could.

CHAPTER 8

I snapped myself out of shock and looked around the room. Had anyone heard his body fall? There were no footsteps on the stairs that I could hear, and no hushed voices.

I came to my feet and stepped over Wagner's body, grabbing my handbag as I walked out of his living quarters and toward his offices. I stopped at the landing to make sure I couldn't hear anything unusual, and then I hurried across to the table where the maps were laid out. While I studied the pins and notes and small figures placed all over Europe, I took my knife attached to a garter from my bag and slipped it over my shoe and up my leg so it rested tightly around my thigh.

I committed every bit of information to memory, and then moved to his desk, rifling through drawers. The top of the desk was clear, and most of the drawers were empty. But there was a locked drawer on the bottom right side and I dug in my handbag for the lipstick.

My head jerked up as I heard noise from below, and my fingers trembled as I went to work on the lock, fumbling in my haste. When the lock snicked open, I jerked open the drawer and saw a brown leather satchel inside. I grabbed the whole thing and strapped it over my shoulder, tightening the strap as much as I could around my small frame.

I took off my shoes and left them under the desk, and then I headed back to the landing and the stairs. My pulse beat rapidly in my throat as I considered my options. There had to be a passageway from Wagner's rooms to the servant stairs, but I didn't know where it was. There were several bookshelves and a fireplace, and it was likely the entrance to the servant stairs was behind one of those, but I couldn't waste valuable time trying to find the entrance.

I had no choice but to go back down the main stairs and go through the kitchen to the servant stairs. From there, I was hoping I'd run into the Alliance and the secret room that held the Cordiers.

I slid my knife from the sheath and padded down the stairs softly. Whatever noise I'd heard earlier would have dire consequences, and I saw the first body of one of the officers who'd been charged with guard duty lying at the bottom of the stairs. His arms were splayed wildly above his head and his eyes were open and staring straight at me.

I paused when I got a better look at his face, realizing that this man hadn't been one of the two who'd been standing at attention when I'd first arrived hours earlier. If what Wagner had said was true and he did have eyes and ears inside the Smithers' home, then he'd have planned for an ambush tonight.

There were two other bodies at the front of the house, and I felt my heart stop as I realized one of them was John Armstrong. Blood trickled from the corner of his mouth, and the hilt of a knife stuck out from his neck.

We'd found an accessible entrance point on the blueprints from the roof onto a fourth-floor sunroom, and as far as I knew, that was how the team planned to infiltrate the house. Whatever had happened down here had passed, and they'd moved to a different location. I just couldn't quite figure out which direction they'd gone. The officer at the bottom of the stairs could have been blocking them from coming down or chasing them up.

I cleared the area before moving past the stairs and toward the kitchen door. It was a swinging door, but it was perfectly still. I pressed my ear to the door and heard nothing but silence, and then I carefully pushed the door far enough that I could see into the kitchen.

There was a soft thud as the door hit something solid, and I pushed again. Something heavy blocked the door, and I put all my weight behind it, pushing until I could squeeze through the opening and over the body of another officer.

The guys had been outnumbered, but where the Gestapo was used to brute force, the Alliance had spent time honing life-saving skills and stealth. The officer at my feet had a broken neck, as did a second one who was crumpled close to him.

I held the knife in my hand so it was concealed from anyone approaching me, and I hoped the sight of a scantily clad woman would be enough to give me a moment's advantage if I needed one.

The kitchen was basic in function with a long counter that ran down the middle, and I skirted around the edge until I reached the door for the servant stairs. My hand rested on the black iron knob and I turned it slowly, pushing open the door.

We had no intelligence on the servant stairs or where they led or how they were accessed from the other room. It was a barren area with wooden steps and no carpet. It was narrower than the main stairs and there was draft that whistled down the cramped maze. The walls were papered in a small floral print that looked thin and worn, and dim sconces barely provided enough light to see one step in front of the next.

I heard nothing as I started to climb the stairs. There had to be a hidden panel some-where along the wall. Homes along this stretch of road predated the Revolution, and secret passageways and hidden rooms were *de rigueur* during those days.

I trailed my hand along the wall as I made my way up the stairs, and I touched something wet along the way. When I held my fingers up to the light, I could see the red tinge, and when I brought it to my nose, I could smell the coppery scent of fresh blood.

I somehow knew it belonged to Graham, and I placed both palms along the wall, feeling for seams to a hidden doorway. Four steps up I found exactly what I was looking for. The papered section looked just like the other wall panels, but this one felt different. The gap between panels was just a hair wider.

And then I heard it. Just a small sound at first—what sounded like a grunt—and I pressed my ear against the wall. It came again. Louder this time, and I recognized the sounds of fight-ing. I couldn't find the lever to open the door, and I couldn't remember ever being so scared as

I was at that point. I knew it was Graham on the other side of the open door.

He was a man with honor, a man who'd let nothing get in the way of his mission except for death. And I knew in that moment I couldn't lose him. I wanted the chance for a future, and for that to happen we had to make it out alive.

I tamped down my panic and sucked in a deep breath, letting it out slowly, and then I ran my fingers over the wall again, starting at the bottom and working my way up. Once I got to the point where I could no longer reach, I moved up a step and kept feeling for the anomaly I knew had to be there.

There were more muffled sounds from the other side, and I went up another step, stretching farther this time. And then a third step. I was barely able to reach across the top seam of the door, and then I felt it. Just a small button that would've been much more reachable for a man or a taller woman.

I pressed the button and there was a click as the door swung inward and a whoosh of dank air and light hit me in the face. The light was stronger than it was in the stairwell, so I blinked several times so my eyes could adjust to the change.

At first I didn't realize what I was seeing. And then I hesitated, not believing what I was seeing. Graham and Auguste were locked in close combat, blood pouring from Auguste's face and a wound that was bleeding badly on Graham's shoulder.

Behind the fight, someone had built bars from floor to ceiling, caging in the Cordier family. Or what was left of them.

"Run," Graham said, landing a punch in Auguste's midsection. "He's a mole."

It made sense that it would have to be someone deep in the Alliance. The information he'd have been able to share with Wagner would have been invaluable. I didn't know what to do or how to sway the fight in Graham's favor. I'd have given anything for a gun, but the space was small and things were happening so quickly it would have been a risk to pull the trigger.

I still held my knife in my hand, tucked behind my arm so it was concealed, but I felt woefully underdressed for the occasion, in more ways than one. I saw Auguste pull a knife from the sleeve of his coat and I gasped, moving forward as if I could have stopped him with my presence.

It felt like a vacuum inside the secret room, and the air rushed from my lungs and my heart pounded in my ears. There was nothing I could do. The silver of the blade flashed as Auguste drew back his hand, but Graham blocked him by grabbing his wrist and then pushing with all his might until Auguste slammed up against the wall.

Graham's forearm pressed against Auguste's throat until gasping and gurgling replaced the grunts and groans. Desperation filled Auguste as he fought for breath and his legs and free arm swung frantically, slowing as the seconds ticked by like a windup toy running down.

Eventually Graham stepped back and Auguste's limp body fell to the floor. Graham was bruised and bleeding, but he was alive, and he looked down at his friend with a look on his face I couldn't describe—maybe disappointment—maybe grief.

And then he looked at me and I ran toward him. The sound came rushing back into my ears and I heard the cries and screams of the children locked in the cage.

"Oh, God," I said. "Are you okay?"

"Is Wagner dead?" he asked coldly.

I shrunk back a little at his tone. "Yes," I nodded. "He knew who I was."

Graham nodded, and then quick as lightning he grabbed me by the throat and pushed me against the same wall where he'd killed Auguste. My breath was cut off instantly and it felt like my face was swelling with blood. The lack of air to my brain, and maybe because I was so blinded by what I wanted to be love, was the only reason it took me so long to realize that

Auguste hadn't been the mole. Henry Graham was the mole, and he was cleaning up loose ends and would be going back to MI6 having protected his double agent status. It's why he'd let the others help him kill all the officers before he'd turned on Auguste. And I'd done the dirty work and killed Wagner.

"Beautiful dress," he said, his face contorted and crazed. "You were quite good at your job. I don't want you to die thinking you were a disappointment. But you were playing against a stacked deck. You were always going to lose."

He loosened his grip enough for me to gasp for air and then closed off my passageway again. Spots danced in front of my eyes and the pain in my lungs felt like I'd swallowed hot pokers.

"If it's any consolation, I enjoyed you more than any of the others who've died before you. But these things happen," he said. "It's war. And war is about money and power, and I have both."

Somewhere during his speech I'd resigned myself to dying. I couldn't fight him. He was too big, and I didn't have much strength left. But then he'd made the comment about how he'd done to other women what he was doing to me, and there was somewhere in my brain that took offense to that. I'd never been like other women, and I certainly wasn't going to die like one.

I remembered the knife in my hand, and I

thought of my father and that he'd finally done something good as I jabbed the knife into the soft tissue of his stomach and jerked up with the blade. Just like I'd been taught.

Graham's eyes widened and he released me, taking a stumbling step back and then another. I fell to my knees and gasped in air. If he'd been able to kill me at that moment, I would have been a goner because I had nothing left. But he just stood there, looking down at the green hilt protruding from his belly.

He stumbled back once more and tripped, falling to his backside, so he was half propped against the cage and the wall. Blood covered the front of his shirt and blood dripped from the corner of his mouth.

"Just in case you need the information in hell," I told him. "Never compare one woman to another. We don't like that."

A gray pallor came over his face and the life went out of his eyes. And Henry Graham, the Alliance's most infamous spy and the man who'd made me hope for love, was dead.

EPILOGUE

"Holy smokes," Ada said, her eyes wide and her mouth forming a soft *O* of surprise. "That was certainly not what I was expecting."

"The best stories never are," Scarlet said, giving her a wink.

"Mama is not going to like that you told me that end part. She says garbage in means garbage out," she said, pointing to her brain.

"That's true," Scarlet said. "But I'd hardly call it garbage. I was a hero. I even got a medal."

"I guess that's okay then," she said. "But just in case maybe we should keep this between you and me. I can keep secrets as good as any spy."

"I don't doubt it," Scarlet said, turning the knife over in her hand. The picture in her mind of that day was just as clear more than three-quarters of a century later. She could still feel what it felt like to defend herself and she could still smell the blood.

"Did it make you sad to have to kill him?" Ada asked softly.

"Not really," Scarlet said, and then she decided to tell the truth. "Maybe a little. I thought we might have a future together. There was a time in my life where I thought about having a husband who'd take me all over the world on grand adventures."

"And children?" Ada asked.

"Nope," Scarlet said. "I like wearing fancy dresses and drinking whiskey too much. Children tend to mess up aspirations like that. But I got to have your mama and I get to have you. And that's just as good as having my own children."

"I suppose so," Ada agreed. "I'm sorry you had to kill him. He seemed nice at the beginning of your story."

"Oh, he was a charmer," Scarlet said. "But he had it coming. Though I prefer long-distance killing. A knife is awful messy, and hitting bone gives me the heebie-jeebies. Probably not something you'll have to worry about though."

"I should hope not," Ada said. "What about the Cordiers? Did you save them?"

"I saved the children," she said, frowning. She didn't like to think about Dr. Meissner and what he'd done to those poor babies. It had taken her years to stop the nightmares after the war was over. "Unfortunately, Mr. Cordier had already succumbed to Dr. Meissner's experiments. The children and I were all smuggled out of France just hours later. And it was right in the nick of time. Not two days later the Nazis bombed Marseilles, and hundreds of people were killed and all the homes and businesses along the waterfront were destroyed. It was a horrible time, and the Nazis were horrible people.

Ada chewed at her lip worriedly, and Scarlet forgot how young she was. It was an easy thing to do because Ada was as sharp as a box of tacks and had been reading almost as soon as she'd started talking.

"So they grew up without parents?" she asked. "That must have been horrible."

"I imagine it was for a while," Scarlet said. "But we got them out of Marseille to London, and they were smuggled on a ship to the United States. They ended up with a wonderful family, and they're all still alive today."

"You still know them?" Ada asked, excitement in her eyes.

"You get to be my age you know just about everyone."

Ada nodded as if it were fact. "What happened after you got out of Marseille?"

"They gave me a job."

"A job killing people?" Ada asked.

"Not exactly," Scarlet said. "A job as a full-time spy. On loan, of course, from the American government. I'd stolen a lot of information from Wagner's office, and I'd memorized his maps. I was able to save a lot of people with that information."

Ada's eyes were practically goggling out of her head. "I can't wait to tell Paris Wheeler you were a spy and killed Nazis. Her family is a bunch of good-for-nothings."

Scarlet had known the Wheelers for a lot of years, and she had to agree—they were a bunch of good-for-nothings, so she moved on.

"I felt right at home over there," Scarlet said. "And I was good at a lot of things, like learning a bunch of languages and being sneaky."

"That's true," Ada said. "Granny is always talking about how sneaky you are, and Mama says you need to do a better job of watching your language around me." She screwed up her face and looked at Scarlet quizzically. "Is that the kind of language you're talking about?"

"Kind of. Those words are good in every language, and if you're going to be a good spy you've got to learn all of them. As far as being sneaky, it's in the blood. My daddy snuck around making illegal whiskey for years and never got caught, and your mama's whole business is sneaking around and spying on people."

"I guess I never thought about it that way," Ada said. "I guess that makes me a natural sneak."

"Don't go getting any crazy ideas. You'll know when it's your moment to be sneaky. It'll present itself to you, just like it did to me all those years ago."

Scarlet felt the strain of exhaustion and the weight of memories she hadn't thought of in a long time. "Come on," she said. "Let's go in and have a nap before dinner. Verna is making tacos."

Ada hopped up out of the swing as only someone with youth could do, and then she grabbed Scarlet's hand and helped her to her feet.

"Do you think you could tell me some more stories?" Ada asked.

"About what?"

She jumped up and down in her Mary Janes, and squeezed Scarlet's hand. "Did you kill anyone else? Did you fall in love again? What happened with the war?"

"You should read a history book instead of watching *The Bachelor*," Scarlet told her. "You can find out real fast how it ended."

Ada waved the suggestion away. "I know how the war ended," she said, rolling her eyes.

"We creamed them. I learned all about it on this documentary I saw. I want to hear about another mission. Did Graham ruin you for all men like your friend said he would?"

"Those are definitely questions for after a nap," Scarlet said. "And maybe a highball. I'm going to need some energy to talk about that."

Ada rubbed her hands together in anticipation. "That sounds better than TV." And then she stopped and stared at Scarlet, as if she were trying to see her as she had been so long ago instead of the stooped and wrinkled woman standing before her. And then a look of worry came over her face. "Mama and Daddy are going to call tonight and ask about my first day at school."

Scarlet nodding, understanding where Ada was going with the statement. "How about we make a deal. I won't mention Paris Wheeler if you don't mention the story I just told you. We don't want to upset your mama. It might make the baby crazy."

Ada pressed her lips together. "I don't think that's a thing, but it sounds like a pretty good deal to me. Can I call you Bouncing Betty?"

"Not if you want to live to see first grade."

"How about an extra dessert after dinner?"

Scarlet put her hands on her hips and looked down at the tiny sprite of a girl. "And what do I get?"

"You can have an extra dessert too," she said. "It's a win-win."

"Yep, you're a Holmes all right," Scarlet said, following Ada into the house and letting the screen door slam behind them.

Scarlet's adventures are just beginning! Make sure you check out Hand Grenade Helen, coming June 2021.

ORDER NOW!
Hand Grenade Helen

Whiskey and Gunpowder

Whiskey Lullaby

The Scarlet Chronicles

Bouncing Betty

Hand Grenade Helen

Front Line Francis

The Harley and Davidson Mystery Series

The Farmer's Slaughter

A Tisket a Casket

I Saw Mommy Killing Santa Claus

Get Your Murder Running

Deceased and Desist

Malice in Wonderland

Tequila Mockingbird

Gone With the Sin

Grime and Punishment

Blazing Rattles

A Salt and Battery

Curl Up and Dye

First Comes Death Then Comes Marriage

Box Set 1

Box Set 2

Box Set 3

The Gravediggers

The Darkest Corner

Gone to Dust

Say No More

Liliana Hart is a *New York Times*, *USA Today*, and Publisher's Weekly bestselling author of more than sixty titles. After starting her first novel her freshman year of college, she immediately became addicted to writing and knew she'd found what she was meant to do with her life. She has no idea why she majored in music.

Since publishing in June 2011, Liliana has sold more than six-million books. All three of her series have made multiple appearances on the *New York Times* list.

Liliana can almost always be found at her

computer writing, hauling five kids to various activities, or spending time with her husband. She calls Texas home.

If you enjoyed reading this, I would appreciate it if you would help others enjoy this book, too.

Recommend it. Please help other readers find this book by recommending it to friends, readers' groups and discussion boards.

Review it. Please tell other readers why you liked this book by reviewing.

Connect with me online:
www.lilianahart.com

[f] facebook.com/LilianaHart
[O] instagram.com/LilianaHart
[BB] bookbub.com/authors/liliana-hart

ALSO BY LILIANA HART

JJ Graves Mystery Series

Dirty Little Secrets

A Dirty Shame

Dirty Rotten Scoundrel

Down and Dirty

Dirty Deeds

Dirty Laundry

Dirty Money

A Dirty Job

Dirty Devil

Playing Dirty

Dirty Martini

Addison Holmes Mystery Series

Whiskey Rebellion

Whiskey Sour

Whiskey For Breakfast

Whiskey, You're The Devil

Whiskey on the Rocks

Whiskey Tango Foxtrot

Whiskey and Gunpowder

Whiskey Lullaby

The Scarlet Chronicles

Bouncing Betty

Hand Grenade Helen

Front Line Francis

The Harley and Davidson Mystery Series

The Farmer's Slaughter

A Tisket a Casket

I Saw Mommy Killing Santa Claus

Get Your Murder Running

Deceased and Desist

Malice in Wonderland

Tequila Mockingbird

Gone With the Sin

Grime and Punishment

Blazing Rattles

A Salt and Battery

Curl Up and Dye

First Comes Death Then Comes Marriage

Box Set 1

Box Set 2

Box Set 3

The Gravediggers

The Darkest Corner

Gone to Dust

Say No More

Printed in Great Britain
by Amazon

25543291R00081